# KISSING
# MR. WRONG

## A WRONG MAN STORY

# KERRI
# CARPENTER

Entangled Publishing, LLC
2614 South Timberline Road
Suite 109
Fort Collins, CO 80525
Visit our website at www.entangledpublishing.com.

Lovestruck is an imprint of Entangled Publishing, LLC.

Edited by Heather Howland
Cover design by Heather Howland
Photography by iStock

Manufactured in the United States of America

First Edition May 2015

*For Aimee Freeman - a fantastic mother, coworker, friend, and writer. You're doing a great job!*

# Chapter One

Vanessa knew it happened to other people, but she still couldn't believe it had happened to her. Even after the requisite talk with human resources, then packing up her desk and turning in her work ID, her brain refused to accept it.

But she had definitely been laid off today.

She dropped off her stuff at her apartment, and then went directly to her home away from home, also known as Mike's, the bar downstairs.

Sure, she'd been given her usual cheerful greeting, and the pity glass of Pinot Noir had been delicious. But nothing was making her feel better at the moment. Not even the hot eye candy sitting at the end of the bar, who kept throwing glances in her direction. With his broad shoulders, muscular arms, and ready smile, he was just her type. Only tonight was not the ideal time to flirt. All she could do at the moment was mope.

"Don't worry about it, V," Mike said, leaning over the

bar. "You can work here until you find something new."

Mike's offer was kind, and she had every intention of taking him up on it. Still, she'd thought her waitressing and bartending days were over. Unfortunately, one of the downsides of living in a small Virginia town two hours outside Washington, DC, was that graphic design jobs weren't falling off trees.

*Moving there is a huge mistake,* her mother's disapproving voice echoed in her head. *You'll come to regret it. Mark my words.*

Pushing all maternal criticism from her brain, she offered a small smile. "Thanks, Mike, I really appreciate it." Stealing a quick glance around the large mahogany bar and even larger dining area, she decided it wasn't the worst place to work. She knew the menu inside and out, as well as most of the regulars. "When do you need me to start?"

"Why don't you take a couple days off and start next week?" His eyes held sympathy as he pushed a glass of water across the bar.

"Thanks," she mumbled.

A quick glance at her phone showed her that her best friend hadn't called her back yet. *Come on, Jess, I need you.* Trying not to take it personally, she sighed. After all, she knew exactly where Jess was. Where she *always* was lately.

"What's Jess up to tonight?" Mike asked, as if reading her mind.

She shrugged. "Probably with Paul."

"That got serious fast."

Sure had. If Vanessa hadn't been in such a sour mood, she would admit how happy she was for her friend. Jess had been the first person to befriend her when she moved to Crescent Falls two years ago for, ironically, her new job. Now, her old job. She blew her overgrown bangs out of her face. She really needed to do something about them soon.

"So what do ya say, V? Want another drink?"

As a matter of fact, she did. But the tears that kept pushing at the backs of her eyes, oh, those waterworks would start full-force if she opted for a second glass of wine. As it was, the Pinot Noir she favored tasted like ashes in her mouth. Fitting, she supposed, since her dream job had gone up in flames today. She pushed the half-full glass aside and opted for the water.

She couldn't help but notice that while the hot guy at the end of the bar kept his hand wrapped around his own half-consumed beer, he seemed intent on her answer as well.

"Nah. This is it for me. I should be heading out soon anyway."

"Okay." Mike shot her a relieved look. Yeah, she knew he didn't do well with weepy women. "I really am sorry. You okay getting home?"

Unable to suppress it, she rolled her eyes. "I think I can make it all the way upstairs just fine."

Mike grinned. "You know I have to ask."

"I know, I know. Thanks, Mike. I mean, boss." When she tried to pay her tab, Mike waived her off. She was too tired to put up a fuss.

On her way out of the bar, she passed the door that led to the landing of the apartments above and paused. She could go upstairs and pick up her paintbrush. Art had always been an outlet for her and maybe she could take some of this sadness out on the canvas.

No. Art *used* to be her outlet. Lately, it had only added

to her frustration.

Maybe she could go upstairs and put on a weepy movie. She wasn't drunk, but she was definitely emotional.

The thought of going to her cramped apartment for a private pity party... Nope. No way. She needed air. Lots of it.

Outside, the recently fallen leaves crunched beneath her black boots. She inhaled, taking in the distinctly autumnal smell that always reminded her of fires crackling away in hearths, Friday night high school football games, and the remnants of Halloween candy.

The fact that a tiny town in the middle of nowhere had become home still surprised her. Thanks to Jess, her old job, Mike's Bar, and the other friendly residents, she'd come to love it. Even without a nightlife, or many job possibilities that didn't involve manual labor or horses, she still adored living there.

Vanessa didn't have to think about where she wanted to go tonight. She crossed the street and headed for one of her favorite spots.

The old stone bridge across from the bar dated back to God-knew-when. Probably Revolutionary times, she thought, as she leaned over the edge and listened to the bubbling water below. The sound of the water running over the many rocks she knew were down there calmed her. Brought her peace.

She hopped up and swung one leg over the side, intending to sit a while before returning to her apartment.

"No, don't!"

Freezing at the loud, insistent voice, she chanced a glance over her shoulder. It was the hot guy from the bar. Only he looked less hot, more worried, as he quickly approached her with both hands held out in front of him.

"Please don't."

"Don't what?" she asked, confused.

"Trust me, it's not worth it. I know you had a shitty day. Believe me, I've had my fair share. But you'll find a new job."

Cocking her head, she took in his concerned expression. Not to mention the incredibly muscular body, held so tightly in anticipation that his dark green polo shirt strained against it. As he slowly neared, she realized he was even taller than he'd appeared while seated in the bar. If she was five-eight, he was probably an inch or two over six feet, but his rippling muscles, square jaw, and broad shoulders made him seem much larger.

Close now, he stretched a hand toward her. "Please, give me your hand."

He had light eyes, either green or blue—she couldn't tell in the dark. But she could detect the fear...and that's when it hit her.

"Ohmigod!" she cried. "You think I came out here to jump?"

He inched forward another foot and was close enough now that she could determine his eyes were, in fact, a light blue. His hair was brownish-blond, and cut incredibly short. It seemed soft, and she wondered what it would feel like to rub her hand over it.

"Didn't you?" he asked, his jaw ticking.

"Of course not."

Lowering his hand, he frowned. "I'm sorry. I just assumed."

Yeah, but... "What are *you* doing out here?"

"In all honesty, I followed you." He nodded as if that

were a completely normal and totally non-stalkerish thing to say. "I overheard you saying you lost your job and saw that you'd had a glass of wine. It seemed like you and the bartender were tight, so I was confused when he let you leave upset."

Wow, someone was observant. Observant and accurate. "Mike's a great guy. But he wasn't worried because I literally live in one of the apartments above the bar." She pointed back toward the building that held Mike's Bar—and her apartment—to prove it.

"Ah."

Under the glow from the streetlamp, she could tell his cheeks were turning a soft shade of red and decided to be nice. Besides, it had been a very long time since someone had worried about her well-being. It felt nice to know someone cared.

That must be why butterflies were dancing around her stomach as she continued to stare at his handsome face. And, okay, she may have taken another glance at his well-defined chest. She was only human.

"Thanks for…being a gentleman," she decided.

He grinned, fast and brief, and her heart stopped. Wow, just wow.

"You're welcome."

He closed the final distance between them and stuck his hand out again. "My name's John. I heard the bartender call you V?"

"It's just a nickname. My name is Vanessa." She slipped her hand into his, and his large, warm fingers curled around hers. The sensation had her breath catching in her chest as her eyes shot up to meet his. His face mirrored her startled expression.

Realizing she was still straddling the wall, Vanessa tried to swing her leg back over to the bridge side. But she was so enraptured by John's rugged face, his mesmerizing touch, and his amazing body that she slipped. There was only enough time for a scream to escape her lips before she went over the side of the bridge.

• • •

Every bit of training John had gleaned from his six years in the Army, not to mention the four years of ROTC in college, kicked in full force.

As soon as Vanessa had gone over the bridge, his arm had shot out faster than rounds from the M4 he carried on a daily basis in Afghanistan. His next step had been to secure his grip on her arm, all while maintaining eye contact.

Even with his heart pounding in his ears, he steadied his breathing and spoke in a clear, calm voice. "It's okay. I've got you."

With her face drained of all color, the dark, intoxicating eyes he'd noticed earlier looked even larger. He could see her chest rising and falling as she sucked scared breaths into her lungs. But she surprised him when she nodded, squeezed his hand, and said, "Okay."

Using all of the strength he possessed, he tightened his grip. Pretty soon, he had both hands wrapped around hers, and began pulling her up and over. When her knees cleared the wall, she let out a cry. John held his breath and steadied himself for the full brunt of her weight. As soon as her feet met solid ground, she fell into him.

"Are you o—"

He couldn't get the sentence out before she flung her arms around his neck, holding on for dear life. While it may have started as a means to steady her, when he held her tightly against him, running his hands up and down the length of her back, he knew he wasn't just calming her. He was reassuring himself that she was alive and well. She hadn't fallen off the bridge.

She was safe.

John recognized the adrenaline pumping through his body. He'd experienced the sensation more times than he could count during both tours overseas.

Realization hit hard, just as it had that day in Afghanistan when everything went to shit. This had been his fault. He'd seen her on the bridge and his mind went right into crisis mode. She probably would have been just fine if he hadn't butted in. His assumption had ultimately caused her to slip and almost go over.

He'd tried to play hero. Again. And in the process, he almost came out as the villain.

Again.

Pushing thoughts of Afghanistan, and that wretched night with his unit, aside, he turned his thoughts back to the woman cowering in his arms.

He could feel every curve of her body. Where was her damn coat anyway? She should definitely have a coat on, with how cold the night had become.

And then there was the scent of her dark hair—something flowery, like roses. It tickled his nose.

"You're okay. Everything's okay," he whispered into that black hair. His voice sounded gruff, and he wasn't sure if it was from the exertion of pulling another human being over a centuries-old stone bridge, or from the way her body was forcing his to wake up.

"I can't believe that just happened," she said. "I'm sorry."

He took in her dark brown eyes, large with fear. "What are you sorry for?"

"I have no idea." She half-laughed, half-choked. Then her lips turned up slightly at the corner. "I needed to say something."

"This was entirely my fault," he said. "There's nothing for you to be sorry for."

"It was an accident. I didn't think about how dangling my legs over a bridge might seem to someone else. In the end, you saved me. You're a hero."

"No," he said, loudly and definitively. She winced and he quickly reined in the emotions the word *hero* brought up. "I mean, I'm just glad you're okay."

"Me, too."

God, she was beautiful. Dark lashes surrounded her gorgeous eyes. Eyes the color of onyx in a face made of pure alabaster. Not a single imperfection marred that skin. Her thick hair was long, and framed her face in layers of luscious waves.

"What?" she said on a breathy sigh.

"You're beautiful."

Her cheeks instantly reddened, but she didn't break eye contact. He respected that.

"You're not exactly hard on the eyes either." To prove it, she ran a finger along his jawline. Her light touch sent a delicious tingle down his spine. His reaction was to pull her even closer, but she kept her head high and he could feel her sweet breath against his neck.

His heart sped up again. She was tall—one of his favorite traits in a woman—and she fit just right with his body. He couldn't seem to look anywhere but at her lips. Lips that were a soft red. Lips that parted seductively as he continued to stare.

Lips that, before he knew it, called to him louder than anything he'd ever heard.

Ignoring every good manner he'd been taught growing up, and all of the training and patience he'd learned in the Army, he framed her face with his hands and kissed her.

# Chapter Two

Vanessa never did things like this.

In fact, she considered herself as boring as they came. She worked hard, paid her bills the second they came in, and always folded her laundry when it came out of the dryer. If there was a rule out there, she followed it.

But tonight, she was suppressing that Goody-Two-shoes and doing something her body was craving more than oxygen.

Maybe it was the adrenaline from almost dying. Maybe she could blame it on getting laid off. Hell, it could be the full moon. In any case, she didn't care. She wanted this guy and she wanted him now.

So she accepted John's lips against hers. In fact, she pulled him closer as she moved her mouth over his. She might not know very much about this guy, but so far he'd proven that he was brave and strong. Plus, the man could kiss.

She wanted to purr, but settled for a soft sigh and ran

her hands down his back until they rested over his ass. He responded by nipping her bottom lip and sucking it into his mouth.

She shivered. The kiss was amazing. It managed to both soothe her frayed nerves and elicit new, tingling emotions.

When he moved his mouth to her neck, she thought her legs would turn to Jell-O, and felt herself slipping.

He let out a small chuckle. "Hey, where are you going?" Then he tightened his arms around her and continued the assault against her neck, her collarbone, then back up to her jawline.

Until he let out a harsh exhale, she hadn't realized that she'd moved her hands to his front, and they were currently dancing along his very firm abs, right above the waistband of his pants. Her fingers slipped under his shirt to feel the hard skin and he groaned, grabbing her hair and pulling her to him even tighter.

There was an insistent voice somewhere in the deep recesses of her mind, calling out to her. *This is crazy-sauce. You just met him. You never do things like this.* But funny how the more he kissed her, the fainter that voice sounded. This might not be her typical Friday night activity, but right now she was fine with it.

"We have to go somewhere." His voice rasped out and his breathing was uneven. It had to match her own. Then his eyes widened. "Sorry. I should ask you first. Do you want to go somewhere?" He gave her a quick peck on the lips. "Please, God, tell me you want to go somewhere."

She would have laughed but she was trying to keep it together. His eyes were dark with lust and they were watching her like she was the only woman on the planet.

No one had ever looked at her like this.

He pressed against her and she felt his erection through the snug khakis he was wearing.

No one had ever *wanted* her like this, either.

"Yes," she managed. "My place. Now."

He smiled, but only for a second. Then he was digging in his heels and the lust began to fade from his eyes.

"I have to tell you something that might change your mind about wanting to go to your place. Before anything happens," he said, his eyebrows drawn together.

That didn't sound good. She hesitated. "Okay."

"I have to leave tomorrow. I'm not even supposed to be here today. I was passing through town and thought I'd drop in on someone, but they weren't home." He dug the toe of his boot into the ground and averted his gaze. "Anyway, I'm going to visit a friend and I'll be there for a couple months, at least. I don't know where I'll end up after that, but it won't be here. My life…well, it's kind of chaotic at the moment."

Vanessa blinked. Given her recent change in employment status, she understood chaos all too well.

"So I didn't want you to get the wrong impression," he said, finally meeting her eyes. "I'm not one of those guys."

This would truly be a one-night stand, she realized. Something she'd never done before. But if she was being honest, she'd had fantasies.

John could fulfill one of those fantasies.

Without going through her usual drawn-out thought process, she went up on her toes and kissed him long and hard. That initial passion she'd felt flared back to life.

"Are you sure it's okay?" he murmured against her lips, even as his hand slid through her hair to draw her face closer to his. If there was any doubt left, the soft strokes of his tongue against hers quickly made up her mind. But then he tore his lips from hers and asked, "Are you buzzed? Drunk?"

Her heart melted at his continued concern for her well-being. She grinned and shook her head. "No, I'm not drunk or buzzed. I know what I'm doing."

Without waiting for a reply, she grabbed his hand and pulled him across the street. She was already breathing hard, and it wasn't from running. She fumbled in her pocket for her key and slammed it into the lock, with John's lips on the back of her neck and his talented fingers caressing her stomach. The door swung open, and they tumbled into the entryway of her building.

*My turn.* She pushed him up against the row of gold mailboxes and practically climbed his body in an effort to kiss him everywhere.

Her lips traveled up his neck. Vanessa heard his breath catch and felt his fingers fist at the bottom of her shirt. She smiled to herself. *Good.* He yanked her shirt from her jeans and ran his hands—rough, calloused, but oh-so-delicious hands—over her skin until they found the front of her pants. Quickly, deftly, he undid her jeans and slid his hand inside. A single finger stroked her through the silky fabric of her panties.

She was going to die. She was going to melt. She was going to explode.

And she'd never look at the mailboxes the same way again, that was for sure.

"Inside. We have to get all the way inside," he groaned.

*Yes, yes, get inside me.* Then she realized he meant in her apartment. That's when it dawned on her that they were standing in the entryway of her building where any of her neighbors could find them at any second. And *then* it dawned on her that instead of feeling terrified they'd be caught, she felt *sexy.*

"Come on," she said, yanking him upstairs while her brain echoed, *come, come, come.*

Somehow they made it up the stairs and into her tiny apartment. Her mind stumbled for a moment—had she done the dishes and vacuumed that morning?—but then John's lips on her neck and his hands sliding under her blouse blanked out her ability to think. There could be dirty laundry and dishes strewn all over the house for all she cared. She hastily unbuttoned her blouse and threw it to the floor.

Moonlight streamed in from the large windows on the other side of the room—enough light that she could see that he was watching her the way a wild animal stalked its prey.

She shivered.

"Come here."

Not that she had a choice. He slid his hands around her waist and pulled her close. Close enough to feel the firm ripple of abs beneath his shirt.

That soft cotton material was really in the way.

She snatched the bottom of his shirt and pulled it up over his head. God, a chest like that should be illegal. She'd heard the phrase "washboard abs" before, but it hadn't made sense until that moment.

The feel of John's hands sliding her jeans down over her hips snapped her out of her blatant ogling, and the intense need to get him as naked as she wanted to be overtook her. She undid his pants and tugged them, and his boxers, down with a grace and speed that surprised her, then stepped out of her own jeans.

He grinned. "Easy there, tiger." One hand slid up her back and deftly unhooked her bra. The other slid her panties down to join her jeans on the floor. He stood in front of her, his naked body gleaming in the moonlight. His eyes roamed over her exposed flesh, which responded by breaking out in goose bumps. His fierce expression was enough to make her thighs clench and other areas of her body *seriously* take notice.

John wasn't the only one looking. Vanessa drank in the sight of his muscled body. Her heart hammered in her chest as her gaze slid down his broad shoulders and rippling stomach to the lean V of his hips. When her eyes reached his bulging erection, she shivered again.

"You still up for this?" John's voice brought her back to reality.

*Up.* Holy hell, yes, she was up for this. And from the looks of things, so was he.

She pulled his face to hers and kissed him. His lips parted beneath hers and she slid her tongue inside, exploring the soft warmth of his mouth. His hands seemed to be everywhere at once, touching, caressing, kneading. When they finally broke apart, she had to gasp for breath.

John smiled, his eyes crinkling around the corners. "I'll take that as a yes."

Vanessa nodded. "Yes, yes, god yes. Just stop talking and put your hands back on me."

*Had she really just said that?*

His smirk and cocked eyebrow confirmed her fears.

But still, he did nothing.

With a groan, she took his left hand and placed it on her

breast. His fingers sought out the sensitive bud of her nipple and her groan became a moan. She took his right hand and placed it between her legs. He wasted no time in obliging her, plunging first one and then two fingers inside her while his thumb stroked her sensitive nub. Vanessa's knees went weak.

Screw what she'd just said. She couldn't believe what she'd just *done*.

"Just needed to be sure," he whispered, his breath hot against her neck. "God, I want to be inside you."

"Please," she gasped. And then his body heat and all that delicious skin were gone, leaving her chilled in the cool air. He pulled a condom from his pocket and turned, his gaze searing a slow path from her head to her toes and back again.

As hot as his gaze left her, she needed him and she needed him now, damn it. She snatched the condom from his hands. "Let me do it."

He chuckled, a dark seductive sound. "Be my guest."

She ripped open the packet and slowly rolled the condom over his hard length, relishing the feeling of him in her hands. Need pooled hot and low in her belly.

John wasted no time backing her up against the door, pinning her body between his and the smooth wood. He hooked her leg up and plunged inside her. She arched and moaned, his full length inside her. He covered her mouth with his and let out his own desperate, primal sound.

"Okay?" he said.

"Mmm," she whispered, still getting used to the feel of him—strong and powerful—stretching her in a way she'd never felt before.

He began moving slowly at first, allowing her body to accommodate his. But every slow, silky thrust built something inside of her. And soon she knew she needed much more.

"Harder," she said against his lips.

With a grin, he obliged, pushing up to fill her even more completely. She gasped and he grabbed her other leg, anchoring her against the door and pumping his hips in a fast, hard tempo.

For the first time in her life, Vanessa saw stars. Sparks crackled across her skin and pressure built deep inside her. Unbelievably, his rhythm picked up even more and Vanessa realized she was close. Very close.

"John…"

"Me, too," he said.

Then she couldn't say anything else. Her body let go, and a tidal wave of sensation soared through her. She let out a long moan just as John gave one final push inside her.

She couldn't breathe and didn't care if she ever did again. All she knew was that she'd just experienced something truly amazing with this man.

A man she'd only met an hour earlier, and likely would never see again.

# Chapter Three

THREE MONTHS LATER...

"Are you sure you're still up for planning my engagement party?"

Vanessa took a sip of her latte and licked away the frothy vanilla foam that dotted her upper lip. She was hanging out at Jess's townhouse, surrounded by an array of colorful throw pillows and ornamental candles. An interior designer, Jess was always changing up the décor with all of the samples she received from vendors. "Of course I'm up for it. Are you crazy?"

Jess kept her gaze glued to her mocha. "I just don't want you to think I'm taking advantage of you."

Vanessa reached across the table and squeezed her friend's hand. "That's what best friends are for. Besides, I'm also the maid of honor. Other than the bride, I'm, like, the most important person in the whole wedding."

Jess gave her a small smile. "True. And I promise not to make you wear something heinous."

"Yeah, yeah. That's what they all say right before the ruffles come out."

Jess laughed and Vanessa was glad to hear the sound. Despite being engaged, Jess had been acting kind of down lately. Vanessa didn't think anything of it at first, but the somber mood just wasn't like her usually lighthearted friend.

It had been that sweet nature and fun-loving personality that had drawn Vanessa to her in the first place. Moving to Crescent Falls had been beyond difficult. She'd had no support from her always-critical mother, didn't know anyone, and had been scared out of her mind to try something new. But she'd met Jess in a particularly bad hot yoga class. The petite blonde was a bundle of energy and helped Vanessa see that everything would be fine. She'd truly become her family over the last two years.

"Anyway," Vanessa said, twirling the almost-empty cup in her hand. "This is one of the easiest things I've ever planned. You know exactly what you want," she said, ticking items off her fingers. "You reserved the space, sent the invites, and picked out the food already. Now it's only a matter of seeing to the little details. No sweat."

Biting her lip, Jess nodded. But she didn't seem convinced.

"Your brother is still going to help, too, right?"

"Supposedly." Jess rolled her eyes. "I mean, if I ever hear from him again. Getting in touch with Jack is like trying to nail down Santa Claus."

Vanessa chuckled. "He's not that elusive. Besides, isn't his deployment over?"

"Yeah." Jess's voice held a note of wistfulness.

Vanessa set down her cup. Her friend should be relieved her brother was out of the Army for good. So why didn't she sound happy?

"What is it?" Vanessa asked softly.

Jess threw her hands up in the air. "You'd just think that if a guy had been deployed for two years the first place he'd want to visit would be—" She stopped herself and grabbed her mocha, but didn't actually drink it.

Ah, now she got it. Jess loved her little brother, but as far as Vanessa knew, he didn't keep in touch. Part of it was probably just the fact that he was a guy. Not to mention that he'd been overseas since right before Vanessa moved to Crescent Falls. She'd never even met him.

One time she'd asked to see a picture of Jack and she would never forget the pained expression on Jess's face. Their mother had died when their house burnt down a couple years ago. The fire had destroyed everything. Pictures, mementoes, all of their childhood memories. Jess moved to Crescent Falls for a fresh start, and since their dad wasn't around, it was just Jess and Jack now.

"Who knows," Vanessa piped up. "Maybe Jack is somewhere debriefing or whatever. I don't know what goes on in the military."

Jess rolled her eyes. "He's probably partying in Vegas or golfing in some amazing location or drinking alcohol out of a coconut at a swim-up bar."

"After serving in the Army for all those years, I think he's probably entitled to a little R and R," Vanessa said. She grabbed Jess's hands again and gave her a light shake. "The important thing is that he's coming home for your engagement party."

"Would be nice to have an arrival date."

"He's going to be here. And until G.I. Joe returns, I've got it covered."

Jess smiled. "Fine, make me feel better. Speaking of G.I. Joe, I know it's kind of crazy to ask a super alpha military man who has absolutely zero experience with engagement parties to help, but I just... I want him involved, you know?"

Vanessa took the last sip of her drink then threw it in the trash. "Maybe we'll use camo-colored balloons for the decorations."

"Ha. Ha. Very funny."

"Tell me something else about your brother."

"I don't know. He's two years younger than us."

"Okay." She waited but Jess didn't continue. "And...?"

Jess made a face. "Fine. Even though he's younger, all of my friends had crushes on him in high school. Talk about gross."

Vanessa laughed. "What's so disgusting about that? You always tell me how handsome he is."

"You don't have a brother so you won't understand. But trust me, the idea of one of your friends getting with your brother is just repulsive."

"Well, don't worry. I promise not to crush on your brother when we meet."

"That's all I ask." Jess finished her coffee drink and then eyed Vanessa. "Speaking of hot hookups..."

"Were we?" Vanessa reached for one of the fresh blueberry scones which she'd brought along and popped a small bite into her mouth.

"We are now. What about that hot guy from a couple months ago?"

*You mean the hottest one-night stand of my life?* Vanessa choked on her scone and coughed. "What about him?"

Jess's eyes bugged out. "Have you heard from him?"

"No, and I don't want to. I mean, I don't expect to. I mean…" She shook her head. "It was a one-night thing and that's it."

She brushed her long hair over her cheek, hiding her face from her friend. To be honest, she really was okay with a one-night stand. Mostly. It was just that she'd never had one before. In all her fantasies, she'd assumed you had sex and moved on.

But the "moving on" part wasn't how it was going down for her.

In fact, she couldn't *stop* thinking about it. About *him* — the incredibly hot guy who'd given her pleasure like no one else in her entire life. Not her high school boyfriend, not her college boyfriend, not even that guy from the dating website who she'd been involved with a couple years ago.

All it took was for her to close her eyes and she could see those penetrating blue eyes, that quick but devastating smile, and those muscles. My God, the muscles.

Not to mention the way he'd moved his long fingers over her skin. She let out a little shiver now.

"Are you cold?" Jess asked.

Warmth filled Vanessa's face. Definitely not cold. "No, I'm fine."

"Are you sure you don't want to call that guy? You could bring him to the wedding."

"No. I mean, yes." Laughing, she shook her head. "Yes, I'm sure, no, I don't want to call him, and *definitely* 'no' to bringing him to your wedding. And I couldn't, even if I wanted to. We didn't exchange numbers." Or last names.

It still stung that she'd had sex with someone without knowing his last name. Well, at least they'd been safe about it. Besides, it was hard to be remorseful over something that had felt so good.

Jess arched an eyebrow, pointing one of her sparkly manicured fingers at Vanessa. "You need a hobby. Something to take your mind off the hottie."

"The *hottie* wouldn't be on my mind if *someone* hadn't brought him up in the first place, thank you very much." *Liar.* But if Jess got any sense of how much and how often she thought about her mystery man, her friend would start taking ads out on Facebook to find him.

"Oh, sure he's not." Jess winked at her. "But if I were pretending I wasn't thinking about a total hottie —"

"I'm not —"

"I would keep myself busy," Jess continued. "And I happen to have the perfect thing to keep you occupied." She produced a flier from her oversized designer handbag with a flourish.

"Do I even want to know what that is?"

"I picked this up yesterday. Here." Jess shoved it in her hands.

Vanessa scanned the flier. "Amateur art show," she read.

"This is perfect for you. You can finally show off your talent."

Vanessa didn't say anything, but Jess's faith in her, as demonstrated by her adamant head nod and wide eyes brimming with excitement, left Vanessa feeling both guilty and honored.

"The show's in one month," Jess continued. "You don't

have to pay anything to enter. Your paintings would be seen by other artists, Crescent Fall residents, and gallery owners. What if one of them wants to buy your work? And why wouldn't they?" She pointed at the painting of the beach at sunset hanging above her couch. Seeing it displayed on her friend's wall when she walked into the room always gave Vanessa a boost of confidence and pride.

She *did* have something she was working on. Only it wasn't ready. It wasn't anywhere near ready. What if she entered it and people thought it was awful? No. No way could she put herself out there like that. Whenever one of her college professors gave her a critique, it was always the same thing.

*You have talent but the emotion's not shining through.*

Decision made, she sighed and eyed Jess. Knowing her stubborn friend, she would have to stall for time. "I'll think about it."

"Great. We should start planning which outfits we'll wear to the art show. What piece are you going to enter? And—"

"You're getting a little ahead of yourself," Vanessa said. "I said I'd *think* about it."

Jess pouted, but there was a hint of a smile tugging at the corner of her lips. "Fine, I can see you don't want to talk about art. I can always go back to talking about your one-night stand hottie…"

Vanessa sighed. *Evil, devilish woman.* What would she do without Jess? But two could play at this game. "*Or* we could go back to talking about all the girls that lusted after your baby brother."

Jess narrowed her eyes, even as a smile began to spread on her face. "Touché."

# Chapter Four

It had been a long, long night. And thankfully, her last behind the bar.

After months of searching, she'd finally found a new job. She was set to start on Monday and dreamed of the day she wouldn't have to respond to calls of, "Hey you," and, "Get me another."

Still, the customers hadn't taken it easy on her just because it was her final night. College basketball games between two rivals always brought in a big influx of patrons, and that night had been no exception.

She'd served more dollar beers and baskets of wings than she thought possible. Plus, she'd had to cut off two different men and clean up multiple glasses that were busted during three-point celebrations.

Walking the length of the bar, she retrieved the few remaining glasses. Carol and Beth, the waitresses working the floor that night, had bussed and cleaned the tables in the dining room. After a quick glance at the bar area, she was satisfied that all messes were taken care of.

"V, you all good to close up tonight?"

She smiled at Mike, still grateful he'd given her this job when she'd really needed it…even if she was so dead on her feet, nothing could revive her. "No problem."

"I worry about you leaving late at night."

Always so protective. She checked her watch and mock-gasped. "Almost midnight. Come on, Mike. I live upstairs. I think I can make it out the front door and over three feet to my apartment building door without any incidents."

Vanessa could tell he wasn't satisfied, but she also knew he was anxious to get to his wife and their weekly date night. He hung two recently washed pitchers on the rack above the bar and gave two quick brotherly tugs to her long ponytail. "We're going to miss you here."

"You'll still see me. Just on the other side of the bar. Can't wait," she finished with a big smile.

He returned her smile. "Good to hear. Okay, if you're sure…"

"I'm sure."

"Then I'm outta here." He untied the bar apron he'd been wearing and tucked it under the counter. "Since it's dead, feel free to close up early. Just make sure the storeroom door stays propped open. The locksmith is coming tomorrow to fix that busted lock."

"Took them long enough to get around to it."

"Don't even get me started. Night, V," he called as he headed out the back exit.

Once the bar was scrubbed down, the ketchup, salt, and pepper bottles wiped clean, and receipts tallied, she piled the last of the glasses and mugs onto a tray to take into the kitchen. Dreams of a long bubble bath and a large glass of wine danced in her head. That's when she heard the front door open. Her fantasy bubbles popped and the wine re-corked itself. Damn. Why didn't she lock the door early?

She hadn't locked the door because it would've been wrong, and Vanessa was nothing if not a rule-follower. Damn it.

With a sigh, she reached for her bar apron and retied it. In the dim light, she couldn't make out who'd come in. If it was one of her regulars, rule-follower or not, she was going to kill him. Rivalry games were one thing, but coming in for a last second drink on her final night?

The back of her neck began to prickle, turning into full-on goose bumps as the man neared. She took in his muscular build, strong shoulders, and square jaw.

*No way.* Vanessa shook her head. *No freaking way.*

"Still open?" he asked as he made his way toward her.

If she couldn't believe her eyes, she had to believe her ears. That deep, steady voice was imprinted in the far recesses of her brain. She heard it every time she closed her eyes.

He stopped in front of her, with only the cold, hard bar between them. Was she dreaming?

"Hi, beautiful," he said.

*Ohmigod ohmigod ohmigod.*

Taking a deep breath, she tried to calm herself even as she oscillated between excitement and confusion. "John?" she asked tentatively.

His grin spread and he let out a small laugh. "Yep."

Her heartbeat quickened, and her skin warmed. "What are you doing here?" Damn it. Her voice sounded so freaking breathy. *Way to play it cool.*

"I came to see you." He shuffled his feet. "I mean, I was hoping I'd see you. I went to your apartment first. When you didn't answer the door, I figured I'd start in the place I first saw you. I remember the owner had offered you a job after…" He trailed off.

"Another day and you would have missed me. I got a new full-time job, and tonight is my last night here," she explained. She realized he was still standing with his coat on and she was probably staring at him like she'd never seen a man before. "I'm sorry. Do you want a drink?"

"Wouldn't mind one. Whatever you have on draft," he said as he shucked off his coat and took a seat in front of her.

Grateful to have something to do with her hands, she grabbed a mug, filled it from the tap, and set it in front of him…then proceeded to ogle him, just like the night they'd met. It was official. He was still the hottest man she'd ever laid eyes on.

"It's good to see you," John said, after taking a long pull of his beer. "Really good."

"You, too. But I have to admit I'm a little surprised. What are you doing in Crescent Falls?"

"I know we said that we were just having fun and everything…"

"Yeah," she agreed.

"But I wanted to see you again."

Her heart did a little somersault at his words. His blue eyes shimmered in the low bar lighting and she could tell that he meant it.

"Really?" she asked.

He nodded. "Although, seeing you isn't the only reason

I'm in town. Actually, I have family here."

That must've been why he'd been in town the first time they met. Vanessa wanted to continue keeping her hands busy, just in case she got the urge to reach over the bar and kiss him. So she resumed collecting glasses and tidying up.

"My sister lives here."

That same prickling-hair-on-the-back-of-the-neck feeling that she experienced when John first walked in returned. Vanessa shivered. "That's nice that you came to visit your sister."

"Trust me, I owe her a visit. Besides, she just got engaged."

Her mouth dropped open. It couldn't be...could it? Crescent Falls wasn't the smallest of small towns, but news about engagements, weddings, and babies tended to travel like wild fire. Especially since, working at the bar, she'd been privy to pretty much every bit of gossip. Were there any other women with engagement plans?

Oblivious to her silent freak out, John took another pull from his beer. "You wouldn't happen to know anything about planning an engagement party, would you?"

Ignoring his question, she leaned forward, practically dropping the tray of glasses. "Is your sister named Jess?"

His face lit up. "How'd you know?"

She fumbled the tray and glasses flew everywhere, breaking against the floor and the bar. A shard of glass bounced up and lodged itself into her hand, but she ignored the biting pain because the only thing she could think about was the hot man sitting on the other side of the bar, a concerned look on his face.

Her one-night stand was her best friend's little brother.

• • •

John was the worst brother ever.

He'd missed seeing his sister the last time he'd passed through Crescent Falls, but despite knowing how wrong it was to come to the bar first this time around, he couldn't help himself.

He'd hoped he'd run into Vanessa again. Wanted to run into her. Needed to see her.

What happened between them had been like nothing he'd ever experienced. The entire night had stayed lodged in his brain during the months he'd been away.

Here he was, back again three months later, and there she was, behind the bar this time. Still the most beautiful woman he'd ever seen.

Last time, her gorgeous black hair and flawless skin had immediately attracted him. But it had been her aching vulnerability that nagged him to go after her. Those huge, saucer-like eyes had held so much hurt and sadness—until he'd helped her over the side of the bridge. Then they'd shone with admiration and gratitude. After months of insecurity and even more self-loathing, John had liked the way she'd looked at him.

Never did he expect the added bonus of having the best sex of his life.

Or that the next time he stood in front of her, there'd be glass lodged in her hand and blood streaming down her arm.

"Oh shit, V." John took in the broken glass and, more importantly, the blood, as she stood, unmoving, staring at him with her mouth open in an appealing little O.

Then she pointed her unbloodied hand at him. "You," she said cryptically.

"Me? Never mind. First things first." He skirted the bar and headed toward her.

"You said you weren't coming back." She stood completely still, back ramrod straight, and her voice dripped with questions and confusion. Maybe he was projecting, but was there also a touch of...excitement?

"I didn't think I was, but then my sister got engaged." He frowned. "I'm not staying forever." He reached her and carefully took her hand in his, examining the damage. "This isn't too bad, but we should clean it out."

She continued to gape at him, her eyes wide, and her head tilted like an adorable puppy.

"What?" he asked.

"I can't believe this."

"I've dropped plenty of glasses, don't worry. Do you have a first aid kit?"

"What? Oh, yeah, in the storeroom." She nodded toward an open door at the end of the bar.

He rinsed her hand in the small sink. "Does it feel like there's any glass left in it?" he asked, gesturing toward her hand. Maybe he lingered a little longer than necessary while running his hand over her soft, smooth skin, but he couldn't help himself.

"This is so not good. So, so, so bad," she said, her eyes darting back and forth.

Okay... Maybe she was in shock? Concern took over as he tried to catch her attention. "Don't worry. You'll be just fine. It's only a scratch." He wrapped her hand in a towel and gave it a little squeeze. "I just need some antiseptic and a bandage.

This time, she yanked her hand away from him and held it to her chest tightly, as if she'd just been bitten. Her face paled and she looked to the side.

"What's wrong?"

Her eyes flicked back up to his. Was it his imagination, or did they hold a certain accusatory glimmer? "You told me your name was John."

Weird. "It is."

"But you said your sister Jess is engaged and lives here?" she asked, and he nodded. A deep red flush filled the previously pale skin of her face. "Are we talking about Jess Campbell?" Again, he nodded. "Jess Campbell's brother is named Jack."

He grinned and looked down. Would Jess never stop with the nickname? "My name is John but my family always called me Jack. Sometimes Jacky, but that was mostly to annoy me."

He broke off at the expression on her face. She was glaring at him as her nostrils flared. Never before had flared nostrils turned him on.

"Jack and John are two different names."

"Actually, Jack is a nickname for John. Like JFK. His family called him Jack."

"That is the dumbest thing I've ever heard. Both names have the same amount of letters and besides...ohmigod!" She covered her face with her hands and he was instantly reminded that he needed to finish tending to that cut.

"What's wrong with my name?" he asked.

"You don't realize it yet, do you?" She turned away and then quickly pivoted back. "How could you?"

Enough was enough. "What's going on here? Why are you so upset?"

"My name is Vanessa Hewitt and my best friend just got engaged."

He still didn't get what was happening, but from the line that had just formed between her brows, he had to assume it wasn't good.

"All caught up?" she asked.

"No." After the night they spent together, he'd assumed she was an easygoing, down-to-earth kind of girl. Maybe he was wrong. "So your best friend is engaged and my sister is eng—"

*Sonofabitch!*

"You and Jess, you're best friends?" *Please say no. Please say no.*

"Yep. You're Jess's little brother?"

All those times his sister had told him he'd been adopted came roaring back into his mind. Damn. He'd never wished that to be true more than right this second.

"Guilty," he said, hoping for some light humor. But looking at Vanessa, knew he hadn't achieved it. "Listen, I know this is a little awkward but there's no reason to freak out."

Vanessa started pacing again. "This is so, so, so bad."

"It's not…good," he admitted.

Then they didn't say anything as they stared at each other. The gravity of the situation finally sunk in and he felt his shoulders slump. Things were definitely gonna get weird now. He'd had a one-night stand with his sister's best friend.

*Shit.*

# Chapter Five

"You're my best friend's brother?" She'd already confirmed this but she could still hope that if she asked again, the answer would be different. Or maybe she hadn't heard him correctly.

"Affirmative," he said, a sad smile on his handsome face.

"You're my best friend's *little* brother." She emphasized the word little and she didn't know why. The only thing she knew was that her feelings were teetering back and forth between disappointment and dread.

He straightened and pushed his shoulders back. "By two years. It's not like I'm twelve." He cocked his head. "Or you're sixty," he added.

She began chewing on a fingernail as she thought about the night they'd met. Had he given her any clue to his family? But even as she raced through that magical night in her head, she knew the answer. They'd been so busy, well, getting busy, that family trees hadn't exactly made it onto the agenda.

And the worst part was that she could still feel his arms around her. She could still smell his musky cologne as she nibbled her way down his body. She could still visualize every taut muscle and ripped ab on his amazing body.

Jess was going to *kill* her. In the two years they'd been friends, Jess had talked about her brother all the time and even though she hadn't said it out loud, Vanessa knew their relationship was complicated. Had she just added to the situation?

And hadn't she *just* promised she wouldn't crush on Jess's brother when he arrived?

Well, guess what? She wasn't crushing on him. She'd freaking slept with him.

Her stomach churned. Oh, no. No. It was even worse than that. She hadn't only slept with John, but she'd told Jess *all* about it. Because they were best friends and that's what BFFs did. They'd gone through every minute detail. Everything. From the way they'd ripped their clothes off in her stairwell to how his touch made her feel to how big...

She was going to throw up.

"Vanessa?" John asked. "Talk to me. You're really starting to worry me."

"I told your sister about your penis," she blurted out.

"What?" His voice came out booming and surprised.

"I know, right? Ahhh." She covered her face with her hands, spun in a circle, and then dropped her head on the bar.

"Why would you tell my sister about my penis? Wait, *what* did you tell her exactly?"

That last part held a certain curiosity inherent to males

and their fascination with their special appendage.

"Nothing. I mean, I just told her…*you* know."

"No," he said. "I have no idea."

"Just the usual stuff that girls talk about. Size, length…"

"What?" he choked out.

She threw her arms in the air. "Whatever. Guys talk about their hookups all the time."

"Sure. But I have never once talked about the size of anyone's vagina."

She blinked. Twice. Despite the situation, Vanessa leaned back and laughed. Then she couldn't stop. She laughed until tears started running down her cheeks and John's own laughter joined hers.

After a few minutes, they calmed. "Vanessa," he began, "I didn't realize who you were."

"Of course not." Now she could feel a blush forming on her cheeks. "We didn't really talk that much that night."

"I don't think it would have mattered though."

*Awwwww.* "You don't?" she asked quietly.

He shook his head.

"But Jess—"

"Jess is a big girl. I'm sure she'll be fine with her best friend and her brother hooking up."

This guy clearly didn't understand females at all. It was her turn to shake her head. "She literally just told me this morning that the idea of one of her friends hooking up with her brother was repulsive. Oh God, I'm repulsive."

"Honey, you are about as far from repulsive as it gets."

He moved toward her. Then she felt his strong hand on her back and for a second—only a second—she remembered what it was like to have his hands roam the length of her body. And right or wrong, she indulged in the memory. She could still recall how those skilled fingers worked their magic over her, strumming her like she was a perfectly tuned instrument.

Only they'd both been played. By each other. By the situation.

As much as she wanted to give in, forget about Jess, and have his arms around her again, she knew she couldn't. Not only had she taken part in a one-night stand, she'd done it with someone who wasn't sticking around. And now he was back, and he'd turned out to be the one person on the planet she wasn't allowed to hook up with.

"Um, Vanessa? You're bleeding through that towel. We really need to tend to your hand."

With a big sigh, she straightened. He was right, at least on that count. Silently, she made her way to the storeroom. Where did Mike keep that damn kit? She could never find it when they needed it.

Aha. She spotted the compact white box, grabbed it, and as she turned, she saw John standing patiently in the doorway, the lights from the bar illuminating his killer body and chiseled face. God, he looked like some kind of action movie star or rugged model standing there. All she wanted to do was lick him. And that was a thought she'd never had before. About anyone.

Well, anyone except John.

"Vanessa," he said, his voice gruff. She didn't mean to, but she couldn't help it. She looked down at his pants and saw that despite their situation, he wanted her as much as she still wanted him.

"John," she whispered. Her breath was coming out in

shallow spurts as her chest rose and fell, each inhale pushing her breasts up toward the top of the revealing white shirt she wore for bartending nights.

She'd dreamed about this moment for the last three months. How many times had she closed her eyes and imagined a reunion with the guy who gave her the best sex of her life? The guy who, for one night, made her feel like a woman. Made her be someone she'd always wanted to be.

Now, he stood in front of her, large hands fisted by his side, watching her with those serious blue eyes and kissable lips.

And then it was like the light switch to her brain went off. Permanently.

She closed the distance between them in two quick steps and his lips landed on hers, fast and greedy. Her hands threaded through his hair, anchoring him to her. Then she took and took, needing this. There hadn't been a day that went by over the last three months when she hadn't needed this. Needed *him*.

Every morning, every afternoon—especially when she got the mail—every freaking time she went up and down the stairwell in her apartment building... Were people aware how many times they went up and down the stairs? Every shift she worked at Mike's, he would sneak into her mind. And then, when she stumbled home, exhausted, feet sore, body worn out, his image woke up every tired part of her, from the tips of her pinkie toes to the highest hair on her head. She'd fall into bed and dream of him.

Damn, she'd been craving these lips.

His solid arms tightened, lifting her off her feet. The next thing she knew she was moving through the air as he continued to kiss her, turning, spinning…

*I promise not to crush on your brother when we meet.*

She ripped herself away from his lips, trying to focus. No, they couldn't do this. She couldn't do this. Jess would be really upset.

*Bang.*

A loud sound followed by the recognizable *click* of a lock sliding into place.

Anxiety cleared the lust from her mind, and she remembered where they were. In the storeroom. The storeroom with the tricky door. The door that locked on its own.

*Well, shit.* She was massively lusting after the most forbidden of all people. But that wasn't the worst of it.

They were locked in a room together.

• • •

One look at Vanessa's face and John knew he should back up, untangle himself from her warm, soft body, and give her some space. But he'd be damned if he wanted to budge even one single inch.

Kissing her was like nothing he'd ever experienced. Kissing her felt like the easiest, most natural thing in the world. Kissing her made the simple act of breathing seem hard in comparison.

But her face had paled again, and her eyes had grown wide. He recognized her panic, even before she put a hand on his chest.

"What? What is it?" he asked, his pulse picking up as he scanned the cramped storeroom for threats. The door had slammed shut after he'd picked her up. Other than that, it appeared to be a normal supply room for a bar. A mass of empty silver kegs sat against a back wall constructed of cinder block. Rows of shelves lined both walls with typical bar supplies like boxes of napkins, oversized containers of olives, and gallons of mixers.

A large light fixture hung overhead, emanating a dingy glow. More than one bulb was obviously burnt out. The half-light played over Vanessa, casting her in an enigmatic glimmer.

"The door," she eked out.

"What about it?" he asked, confused.

"It's broken. We're locked in here."

He blinked—once, twice—before he regained his composure. "We can't be locked in." Taking charge, he strode to the door and tried the handle. It jiggled but didn't budge. He pulled harder. Nothing.

"I told you," she said, coming up behind him, her rosy scent invading his space and taunting him. "This door has been wonky for weeks. The locksmith is supposed to come by tomorrow to fix it."

"Someone should have put a sign on it." He could hear the desperation in his voice. But she was close, too close, and he needed some space, or there was no telling what he would do. Top of the list would be to throw her onto the floor and make love to her right here, right now.

"There *is* a sign on it. Employees only. Non-employees aren't supposed to be in here." She reached around him and tried the door for herself, as if, magically, it would work for her. A strand of her hair escaped her ponytail and brushed his face. It might as well have been a bee stinging him on the cheek. He quickly relocated to the other side of the room, near a shelf filled with boxes of those drink stirrer things.

She chewed on her fingernail, seeming to consider the situation as her eyes darted around the room. Then they landed on him. "I'm dumb. We can just call my boss. Hand me your cell phone." She stretched out a hand, her short-sleeved shirt showcasing her tempting white skin. What he would give to nibble from her delicate wrist up to her tantalizing elbow.

"John," she said, tapping her foot.

"What? Oh." His phone, right. Patting his pocket, he frowned. The other pocket was also empty. "Shit."

"What?" she asked.

"I don't have my phone."

"What do you mean? How can you not have your phone? How is it possible for anyone in this day and age to not carry their cell phone?"

He pointed at her. "You tell me. Where's *your* phone?"

She gestured to her short, tight black skirt and form-hugging white T-shirt. "Where exactly would you like me to stash my phone? In my bra perhaps?"

Great. Now all he could think about was her bra. What color was it? What kind of material was it made of? How long would it take him to get it off of her? Judging by the red of her cheeks, she must have realized her mistake as well.

"Where's your phone?" she asked.

"I left it in the pocket of my coat. The coat that is currently hanging on the back of the chair at the bar."

She hid her face in her hands. "I can't be stuck in here with you."

The statement irritated him. Why didn't she want to be trapped with him in particular? Rubbing the back of his neck, he took in her panicked expression. "It's not like you're stuck with the boogeyman."

"No, worse," she whispered, so softly he wasn't sure if he was supposed to hear it. Still, he felt his face fall at her implication.

A quick war waged inside him. Should he save face, or be truthful? In the end, honesty was always easier. "I'm sorry you feel that way."

Her head snapped around and she pinned him with a sincere gaze. "I've never wanted to make out with the boogeyman."

He took a step toward her. "Vanessa."

She stepped in the opposite direction. "No, don't. We can't do this. We can't do anything."

"Vanessa," he repeated.

"I'm sorry, but what happened between us that night... well, it was a mistake and I regret it."

And just like that, his heart fell.

# Chapter Six

God, Vanessa felt like such an ass. And she'd lied. That night hadn't been a mistake. In fact, it had been the best night of her adult life.

As for regret, well, how could she regret something that made her feel so amazing? That night had been the one bright spot in the otherwise shitty events that had recently made up her life.

They hadn't known who the other was. It's not like they'd planned to betray Jess. She'd been upset and vulnerable. And after she'd almost gone over the bridge, their adrenaline had kicked in and every emotion had been heightened. Surely Jess would understand that.

She was already composing a very long and well-meaning apology for her best friend. Even though she would definitely be shocked, Jess didn't hold grudges. If Vanessa simply explained how she was feeling…

Only that wouldn't matter in the end anyway. John wasn't

staying in Crescent Falls. He made that clear the night they met and he'd already said it again tonight. Vanessa didn't want a long-distance relationship. Besides, could you even have a relationship built on a one-night stand? She wished Jess were there to ask, which of course only made her feel worse.

John stirred and she turned toward him. He was watching her with sad eyes, and wasn't that a punch to the gut? She wished she could rewind time and go back to when he looked at her as if he wanted to eat her up. It would be so easy to tell him that she didn't mean it. That their night together hadn't been a mistake. But one of them needed to keep a level head, and it looked like that person would have to be her.

She turned in a small circle before choosing to sit on a large crate in the corner. "Worst case scenario is we're stuck in here until tomorrow morning. Mike always stops in around nine to go through the previous night's receipts."

"I wasn't worried," he said, leaning against the door. His gaze never wavered. Those mesmerizing eyes, the color of the morning sky, watched her every move.

Shifting, she felt something rubbing against her leg and realized her hand was still wrapped up in the towel John used to stop the bleeding earlier. It seemed like that had happened hours ago.

"I can take a look at that now," he said from the corner.

"No," she answered a little too quickly. "I'm fine." She removed the towel and saw that there was, in fact, a piece of glass still stuck in her skin. She tried to maneuver so she could take it out, but doing first aid one-handed proved more difficult than she anticipated.

John let out a long, frustrated sigh then he pushed off the wall, grabbed the first aid kit, and knelt in front of her. "Seriously, V, let me look at it."

Reluctantly, she offered her hand. "There's still a piece of glass. It's just small, I think."

"I see it."

Intently, he examined her hand. Sitting this close to him, she could smell his enticing cologne. It was a fresh, crisp scent that reminded her of having lemonade near the ocean, that mix of citrus and the sea. His eyes were cast down as he held her hand and she couldn't help but notice he had thick eyelashes. With his brows pulled together, he looked to be deep in concentration.

The feel of his skin on hers, even in such an innocent way, sent a shiver down her spine. When he ran a light finger over her palm she thought she would explode. She wanted him so damn much.

After sifting through the contents of the first aid kit, he reached into his pocket and pulled out a Swiss Army Knife. "I need to get that last shard of glass out."

The feel of his breath on her face, and the way his serious eyes locked on hers, had her trembling.

"Don't worry. This won't hurt," he said, kindness in his voice. Clearly, John had mistaken her lust for fear. *Probably better that way*, she mused.

Using the tweezers attachment, it took him a couple seconds to pull the glass from her skin. He quickly applied pressure and then some antiseptic from the first aid kit. Finally, he cleaned the other scratches and then put a Band-Aid over the largest cut, smiling at the Hello Kitty bandages Mike had stocked.

"You're going to be fine." But he didn't let go of her hand. Instead, he studied her fingers as if they held all the answers he needed. "V, what happened between us…"

"Don't," she said.

He held up his other hand. "It wasn't a mistake. At least, not on my end. And I don't regret it, not even when I think about my sister and how she's going to react."

Vanessa pulled her hand away. She couldn't think while he was touching her. To get even more distance, she crossed her legs and tucked them under her, balancing on the box.

John sat down on the floor and looked up at her.

"Why couldn't you be an only child?" she asked, letting her hair out of its ponytail.

"I like your hair down."

He was so sincere, so real, she wanted to melt. Vanessa knew she was in trouble. So she snapped her fingers in front of his handsome face. "John, focus."

Slowly, his grin spread, and the full effect of it was devastating.

"Sorry, but I'm not getting what the big deal is. You're Jess's best friend. It's not like I hooked up with a serial killer." His eyebrow arched. "Right?"

Smiling, she ran a hand through her hair. "Like I would tell you if I were a serial killer. But come on, you have to understand why Jess would be icked out."

"Icked out? Is that even a word?"

"Icky is a word and that's how Jess sees this." She gestured back and forth between them. "How would you feel if Jess hooked up with your best friend?"

He straightened. "I'd be fine with it."

"Oh really?" she asked, ready to call him out on his

bullshit.

"Yeah, really. My best friend's Lance, and he's a great guy."

Vanessa leaned forward. "So you're telling me you would have no problems whatsoever if Lance and Jess happened to kiss?"

"Nope." His jaw ticked.

"It would be just super great if they hooked up and had sex?" she asked with a stoic face. She could hear him inhaling a long breath through his nose and stifled a laugh.

"Jess is an adult," he said.

"So if Jess and Lance did all of the things that we did…on the stairwell, against the mailboxes, up against my door—"

"Stop," he said in a loud voice. "Okay, okay, it's weird and I don't want to think about my sister doing any of that. With Lance or anyone else on the planet."

Vanessa finally let out a giggle.

"In fact, the next time I see Jess I'm going to strongly suggest she reconsider becoming a nun. They still live in convents, right?"

She shrugged. "Don't know. I think there's a reality show about it though."

"So I guess I get Jess's attitude about me dating her friends. Or not dating," he said in a soft voice.

Her stomach clenched. "Yeah, I guess that would be weird for siblings. Even if it does work out." She looked down at the floor and studied the pattern of the wooden planks.

"It's just that…I never really felt a connection to any of my sister's friends."

Her head snapped back up.

"Until recently," he finished.

She was finished, too. In fact, Vanessa was afraid that before the night was over, something was going to come to an end—either her restraint against John's way-too-tempting advances, or her friendship with Jess.

· · ·

John knew he'd made Vanessa uncomfortable. Or at the very least, he'd made her wonder. Good. His plan was starting to work. He wanted to rub his hands together like the villains always did in those old movies.

Except, he was no villain. He just wanted to explore this thing between him and V. He understood his sister's wishes, but dammit, this wasn't about her.

It was about…himself. John let out a long, deep sigh. Ever since he'd gotten back from Afghanistan, he'd been numb. He tried to put on a brave face for everyone, but the truth was that he was shocked he was able to get through the day without losing it.

Hell, sometimes he did. And those days were bad. Really bad.

Feeling like complete shit while every person around him viewed him as some kind of hero was beyond tough. Their adoring eyes watching his every move had become too much for him.

Then one night he came to visit his sister, even though he was sure she would never understand. In fact, he didn't want her to. Even though she was older, he felt protective, and he didn't want her to ever know the horrible things that happened over there.

So he had been almost happy when she wasn't home that night. He'd headed out to a bar, sat on a stool, ordered a beer, and watched the most beautiful woman he'd ever seen walk in.

That night with Vanessa had been amazing, and not only because of the phenomenal sex. Sure, that was a bonus. But the truly remarkable thing about it was that he'd felt real emotions while he was with her—lust, desire, happiness. To feel anything at all was such a welcome change that being with her almost made him break down and sob.

The minute he'd left town the next morning, he'd regretted their mutual decision to move on without any ties. He'd wanted her last name. He'd wanted to see her again. He'd wanted *her*.

When she looked up from the bar tonight, those dark eyes searching his face, he couldn't believe his luck. Truth be told, he didn't know how long he would stay in Crescent Falls or where he'd end up after he left, but he'd planned to return to her apartment while he was home for Jess's engagement party, convince her to go out with him on a real date.

Because those feelings from the night they met had come back the minute he'd seen her again. And John couldn't ignore the power in that. There was something between them.

Now he needed to get Vanessa on the same page.

He could tell that her mind was working a million miles an hour.

"Maybe we should talk more about your sister."

He narrowed his eyes. "Seriously? You want to talk more about Jess?" He couldn't keep the irritation out of his voice. But, hey, if it made her feel more at ease about the possibility of getting to know him better then he was all for it.

Letting out a small laugh, she got up and searched the shelves until she found a pen and one of those pads waiters used for taking down orders. "I meant we should talk about Jess's engagement party. I mean, that's something we were going to have to talk about eventually. Since it looks like we're stuck in here for the night, we might as well get some work done, too."

"The party. Riiiggghhht."

She paused, watching him. "Do you have something against the party?"

"No, of course not. It's just...."

"What?" she asked.

"Basic training didn't really cover engagement party planning."

"Ah." Snagging an old apron from the hook on the back of the door, she spread it out on the cold floor and joined him. "No worries. You're not alone."

*You're not alone.* People had been telling him that for years. Most recently, his superiors, fellow Army buddies, the psychologist he'd talked to a couple times...even Jess over email. But he'd never liked the sound of that one simple phrase so much before.

Oblivious to the effect her words had on him, Vanessa continued. "Jess did most of the hard work for us. Which, of course, is just like her."

"Yeah, it is." He thought about how resourceful and organized she'd been when their mother had died. And strong. "She does a lot for people."

"And doesn't get much back in return."

Surprised, he sat up straighter. "What do you mean?"

Shrugging a shoulder, she studied her Hello Kitty Band-Aid.

"V?"

Her eyes darted around the room before they landed back on his face. "This is really none of my business, John."

Curious, he leaned forward. "What is it?"

"Your sister misses you. She misses your mom, obviously. But I think she feels really lonely."

His stomach knotted. "Yeah, I get that," he muttered. "We don't really have much family. A couple cousins out in California."

"*You're* her family. I understand you've been finishing your obligations to the Army and Jess gets that, too. But you're done now, right?"

He nodded. He couldn't speak through his constricted throat.

"Maybe it's time to come home now."

"This isn't really home for me. Home was Richmond. At least it was until…"

"I know." She reached for his hand and he let her take it. "But Crescent Falls could be home. I think she really needs you."

The air felt thick as he thought about what Vanessa had just said. His sister had always been a rock. It was weird to think of her as vulnerable, or sad, or lonely. He took a gulp of air. Knowing he needed to think on this new information, mull it over, he let go of Vanessa's hand and changed the subject.

"So, tell me about this guy she's going to marry. What's he like?"

Vanessa didn't say anything for a moment. She studied

him intently, and John almost started squirming. They could use her in the Army for sure. But just as he thought he would break, she relented.

"Paul's a nice guy. He's funny and sweet. He really loves Jess. But the whole thing happened pretty fast."

"Five months of dating right?"

"Only five," she said.

"Definitely a short time to get to know someone. It's not that I think you can't have a connection with someone after five months," he said. "In fact, I think most people know instantly when they're going to have a connection." He looked at her soft, pink lips. "An attraction."

He leaned toward her. For a moment, he thought she was going to open to him. She was right there, ready and willing. He could tell. But as fast as it had started, she pulled back.

"Engagement party." Tapping her pen against the pad, she wouldn't meet his gaze again. "Mucho planning to do if we're going to pull this off in three weeks."

He sighed. She was right, so for the next hour, they went back and forth on decorations and signature cocktails, and a whole host of other things he would have never even stopped to think of.

Tearing yet another page off the order pad, she crumpled it up and threw it across the floor. "Still not right." She chewed on the pen and his gaze flew to her mouth. She really needed to stop drawing his attention there. "Maybe we should come up with a theme first," she said.

They'd both gotten comfortable. Well, as comfortable as you could get on the floor of a bar storeroom. Since they'd both been hungry, Vanessa had opened a large jar of Maraschino cherries, a can of olives, and a tub of bar pretzels.

"Isn't the wedding the theme?" he asked, popping an olive in his mouth.

Shaking her head, she gave him a sorrowful look. "If only it were that easy. But you know your sister. She'll need a Great Gatsby theme, or Mardi Gras. Maybe an Old Hollywood motif," she said, biting her lip as she considered the possibilities. "You know, with a red carpet leading into the room."

"Seems really superfluous," he said honestly.

"Most women do go over the top when it comes to their weddings. If it were my engagement party, I'd have it right here."

"Right here? In this storeroom?" he teased. "With a spread of drink garnishes and bar food?"

"Pretty much. Well, not the storeroom part. But Mike could set aside a corner of the restaurant. I'd have my close friends and family."

"Some sliders, fries, fun music."

Vanessa smiled and it lit up her whole face, made those mysterious eyes sparkle. "Lots of toasts and stories."

"A good, relaxing time for everyone. No pressure," he finished.

"To be honest, I'd want the same kind of wedding, too," she said, nibbling on a pretzel. "Something simple and chill, not a lot of people."

"Maybe on a beach somewhere," he added.

"No shoes and lots of tropical drinks."

"I'd want my Army buddies there. They'd like that." He threw a pretzel in the air and caught it in his mouth. Really, it was just a way to distract himself. The mere mention of his Army buddies made the thought that not all of them would be around for his hypothetical wedding come crashing back down.

The way Vanessa offered him a smile proved she hadn't caught on to the sudden sadness threatening to squeeze his heart. Good. He didn't want her to know about any of the bad stuff.

"And I'd want really good food. Not the usual dried chicken and overdone red meat." She sat forward as excitement took over. "And an amazing band."

"With everyone out on the dance floor throughout the whole night."

"Exactly," she agreed, throwing her arms up into the air. Her hand landed on his thigh by accident and they both froze.

Every nerve in his body stood on high alert. Her breath caught, and he thought it was the most beautiful sound. He remembered her making that same sound at another moment, three months ago. A very intense, intimate moment. Even the reminder of it had him drawing in his own hitched gasp.

As they sat there on the dirty floor, under the murky glow of the industrial light hanging above them, he came to a realization. He wanted her. And before the night was over, he would have her again.

She watched him, her eyes growing darker as they stayed glued on his mouth. Was she going to kiss him? *Do it, kiss me*, he willed her. Then she leaned closer to him and opened her mouth. Only the words that came out surprised him.

"Let's get drunk."

# Chapter Seven

She hadn't meant to say those words. Vanessa had meant to plaster herself to John and kiss the snot out of him.

It was all that talk about their perfect engagement parties and weddings. That's what she was blaming her almost-lapse in judgment on. Where did he get off, describing her perfect day? Furthermore, where did he get off sharing his with her?

And, oh man, she'd loved his. In fact, she'd been completely in sync with everything he talked about. No offense to Jess, but the event her best friend was planning was going to rival the royal wedding. Sure, all that fluff and decorations and event planners and tulle was fine and dandy, but kind of overkill in Vanessa's opinion.

A small, intimate ceremony on the beach, with only very close friends and family, followed by dancing under the stars, on the other hand, sounded amazing. Dancing with John under the stars…

"You want to get drunk?"

His deep, curious voice pulled her out of what, she was sure, would have been a fantastic fantasy. "I mean, we don't have to get obliterated or anything, but since we're in this room with nothing to do but plan your sister's engagement party...."

"Right, the engagement party." He rolled his eyes and she tried not to laugh at his pained expression. "When you put it that way, a little booze does sound pretty good. One problem though."

She cocked her head. "What?"

"All I see are empty kegs back there." He pointed to the far end of the room. "And I spotted a ton of mixers on the shelves. But no alcohol."

Her lips twitched as a slow smile began. "Mike actually keeps most of the alcohol locked in a different room in the basement. But I happen to know that the emergency kit is hidden in here."

"Emergency kit?"

She nodded. "There are always nights that make one or more of us want to bash a couple of mugs over someone's head. Instead, the emergency kit is there to save us."

She tried to stand, but wobbled. Tingles pricked at her leg, alerting her to the fact that she'd been sitting on that leg too long and it had fallen asleep. John reached out a hand to steady her, but as soon as their fingers connected, a different kind of tingling began.

Why did his touch have this effect on her? She'd dated her last boyfriend for two years and never once did she feel an iota of what John made her feel with a simple brush of his hand.

"You okay?" he asked.

*No.* She'd never wanted someone like this before. "I'm fine," she lied. "Leg's a little numb, that's all."

"Must be this comfy floor," he said with a wink.

Relieved that he didn't call her out on her second stumble at his touch, she limped over to the shelves. Simultaneously shaking her leg out and moving all the right boxes around, she found the emergency kit exactly where it was supposed to be—nestled inside a large box that Mike had jokingly labeled "nonalcoholic mixers." He'd figured it was the last place someone with a real drinking problem would check.

"Aha." She produced the full bottle of gin—Mike must have restocked recently—and snagged tonic and two plastic cups from another shelf.

Returning to the floor, she poured them both a generous serving. "Ordinarily I do this whole lime twist thing to my G and T's but we don't keep fresh limes back here, so this will have to do."

"I'm not complaining. Cheers." He touched his glass to hers.

She enjoyed the distinctive flavor, which always reminded her of pine trees, as the gin slid down her throat and instantly warmed her core. It only took a couple more sips for that warmth to spread throughout her body and into her extremities.

"You mix a good gin and tonic, even without your special lime twist."

"Thanks. Lots of practice."

Leaning back against a box filled with cleaning supplies, he sipped his drink, never taking his eyes off her. Did he have any idea how appealing he was? When he studied her with those quiet, intense eyes, was he aware her insides became all gooey?

"Even though you mix a really good drink, I know bartending isn't your preferred profession."

She shook her head. "Nope. I'm a graphic designer. And actually, tonight was my last night behind the bar because I finally got a new job."

He grinned. "So you said earlier. That's great."

"Tell me about it." She let out a huge sigh. "Now I don't have to crawl back to my mother with my tail between my legs admitting that I made a horrible mistake by not listening to her and moving here despite her advice."

She paused, her cup halfway to her mouth. As true as the statement was, Vanessa was shocked she'd said it out loud.

John held his cup out to her. "How about a refill?"

"Sure." Anything to get her mind off this man and his uncanny ability to get under her skin.

"I take it things aren't great with your mom."

Vanessa took her time mixing his drink. "We've never really had a great relationship." She handed the cup to him and met his eyes. They were so calming and open. They had the power to make her reveal way too much. "I was never good enough for her."

As always, the admission stung. A sharp pain in her chest made her catch her breath, even as a bitter taste filled her mouth.

"I'm sure that's not true. Did your mom not want you to be a graphic designer?"

"She wanted me to be an artist, but honestly, I don't have the talent."

"I happen to think you're really gifted."

She cocked an eyebrow. "And how, may I ask, would you

know?"

John gathered some of the crumpled papers scattered around the floor and smoothed them out. He pointed to one and then another. "These. While we were talking about Jess's party, you kept doodling. I don't even think you realized you were doing it."

True. She hadn't. Glancing down, she saw her usual array of doodles. Marvin the Martian, a spotted dog, the house she wanted to own someday. But peering closer at one paper, she saw the old stone bridge and realized she'd copied the painting that sat unfinished in her living room.

"V, you're really talented. I mean, I'm no art connoisseur but those are freaking amazing. And you drew them so fast."

The pride shining in his eyes made her heart swell. More than anything she'd love to agree with him. But after years and years of rejections, believing in herself had become harder and harder.

"I'm good, but I never really had enough passion in my paintings. They always lacked that thing that makes someone connect. You know?"

She thought about the half-finished canvas in her apartment. How many nights had she stood there staring at it, willing the feelings to transfer from her heart to the brush? The fact that her subconscious had her drawing it on the old waitress pad tonight only proved that she couldn't break through her emotional block.

"Anyway, it doesn't matter. If I had pursued art, my mom would have wanted me to get an office job. When I lived in Manhattan, she wanted me to move back home to DC. When I was in DC, she talked about how I should get married and settle down. When I was in a relationship, she claimed I was too young to settle down and should play the field."

"Sounds like an indecisive woman."

"A hard-to-please woman is more like it."

"What about your dad? Where's he?"

"Left when I was five."

"Any other siblings? Cousins?"

She shook her head. John frowned. She knew the feeling. After all, she experienced it all the time. How many times did she have to get that jealous feeling in the pit of her stomach when people talked about their brothers or sisters, or had cousins they considered best friends. She had no one. All alone. At least, until she'd moved to Crescent Falls.

Noticing her drink was empty, she began refilling it, along with John's. The alcohol was clearly doing its job of loosening lips. She never told people about her mother. And she definitely didn't talk about her art. Then again, people rarely recognized she could draw, let alone commented on it. John was definitely more observant than most. Maybe that was an Army thing.

"How did you and my sister become friends?" John asked as he accepted his cup. Then he reached for her hand.

She didn't stop him.

"Jess befriended me when I had no one. I'd just moved to Crescent Falls for a job—the job I lost the night we met. Almost instantly, Jess took me under her wing, introduced me around town, and showed me the ropes."

He grinned. "Sounds like Jess."

But it was more than that. Jess provided her with something she'd never really had before. A true best friend, who didn't judge her or insult her. Vanessa knew that Jess would drop everything if she needed her.

That's why the fact that Vanessa had hooked up with her brother—the one person she'd asked her not to get involved with—was horrible. Looking down at their joined hands, her heart fell. Slowly, she untwined her fingers and pulled her hand away.

"My mother warned me that moving here was a bad idea, but I really wanted the job. Not to mention a change of pace," she said to distract John when he watched her clasp her hands together.

"Most people move somewhere bigger when they're hoping for a change of pace," he said with a wry smile.

"I'd already lived in New York and DC. I loved them both, but I never felt like I truly belonged. I wanted to live in a community. You know?"

"You wanted a family."

She smiled but it didn't last. "Exactly."

"That's one of the things I loved about the Army. A sense of family and community. I'd do anything for that family." As soon as the words left his mouth, his posture stiffened and he looked toward the far wall.

That's when Vanessa realized whatever happened in Afghanistan had monumentally changed him, and not in a good way. Here she was complaining being an only child with an overbearing and disapproving mother when he'd been torn away from his family to serve overseas.

Jess had never told her about any of this. Did she even realize her brother was suffering?

"John," she said quietly. Then she reached over and took his cup, putting it and her own out of the way. He may not have a positive reaction to what she was about to say. "Tell me about Afghanistan. Tell me about what really happened there."

Because she had steeled herself against it, his small flinch and locked jaw didn't upset her.

"I don't want you to hear about that. I don't want it to touch you the way it's touched me. No one deserves that."

She scooched closer to him and took one of his hands in both of hers. "I want to respect your decision."

"But?" He raised an eyebrow.

"The thing is…" Could she really say this? It was going to change everything. "I think I might be into you. So I'd really like to know what you've been through."

He frowned. "Because you think you might be into me?"

It was hard, but Vanessa pushed everything else from her mind. She forced out Jess and the fact that this had all started with a one-night stand.

Instead, she thought about John. About her growing feelings for him. Not only the way he made her feel—which was amazing in and of itself—but how she wanted to make *him* feel.

What was it about this man? She'd known him for less than two days, but somewhere along the line, she'd started to consider him an important person in her life.

And important people deserved to hear the truth.

With a deep breath, she met his stare. "No. Because I'm *definitely* into you."

# Chapter Eight

*I'm definitely into you.* John's chest swelled as he took in her serious eyes. He wasn't a dancing man, but boy did he want to get up and bust a move.

Some of the air rushed out of him as she'd asked to hear about his time in the Army, though, and that was enough to deflate his happiness. He didn't want what he'd been through to taint her. He was tainted enough for both of them. "There's a lot I still can't talk about."

"Because it's classified or because you, um, can't imagine talking about it?" she asked, looking tentative.

"Both." He ran a hand over his face. Could he actually go through with this? He hadn't told anyone outside the Army what he'd seen. What he'd done. But the way she looked at him, like she was afraid he'd break apart, and with her hand clutching one of his, he felt like maybe he could open up a little bit for this woman. "I can't tell you what we were doing or what exactly we were looking for over there. But we had essentially finished our required search."

He paused. He didn't say anything for a good, long while. Vanessa didn't push, and he liked that she seemed comfortable with the long silence. In fact, he liked it very much that he could just *be* with her.

After everything that had gone down overseas, he was inclined to get lost in his own thoughts, even during the middle of a conversation. People didn't understand that and often mistook it for indifference or rudeness. He didn't blame them.

That Vanessa seemed so understanding amazed him.

"We were going to head back to base," he finally continued. "We should have headed back to base," he said under his breath.

Another pause, only this time, he felt something on his face and realized that Vanessa had cupped his cheek in her palm. It was the lightest of touches, but the effect was like a punch to the gut. If she hadn't been waiting for him to finish, he'd have leaned into her palm. Encouraged her to touch him everywhere. To warm the parts of him that still went cold when he forced himself to remember that day.

"I had a hunch," he said, maintaining an even tone as his stomach tightened. "Turns out my hunch was correct."

She squeezed his hand. "That's a good thing, right?"

"It would have been. But I hadn't counted on the ambush. There had been no hunch about that. No warning. No way to anticipate."

In no way did he want any part of that war zone to touch her. He shied away from her touch and stood, needing to pace if he was to get the rest of it out.

"I don't know how many guns went off. I don't even

know what kind they were. Or how long it lasted. Or how many people were holding them. All I know is, at the end, six of my own were injured and one... We all considered each other brothers, but one of them..." He ran a hand over his short hair. "This kid was the runt of the group, that's for sure."

"Tell me about him," she said softly.

"Young, fearless, kinda goofy. Way too optimistic for his own good. Annoying little shit." He took a moment because even he could hear the affection in his voice. "The most loyal little... He was like a faithful dog the way he followed me around. He looked up to me."

John could still see his hopeful, excited face every time he closed his eyes.

"We thought the ambush was over, but we, well, we were wrong. I turned around to see a gun aimed right at my head. Only about ten feet away."

He closed his eyes and willed the memories to go away. Willed time to stop and reverse so he could go back and change history.

"Before I even know what's happening, my little shadow jumps in front of me. He takes the bullet. He lost the battle. He gave his life for mine."

Damned if he still couldn't hear it—the gunshots and the screams, the scrambling to get out of there. It had been his fault. He was the leader and his gut led the most loyal kid he'd ever met to his death.

Turning, he looked at the cold wall, studied those gray cinder blocks as if they held all the answers in the world. Too bad he knew they didn't. There were no answers to help him. Nothing to ease the pain he felt when he went to the mother of his fallen soldier's house.

"What was his name?"

He slowly turned around. Of all the things he could have anticipated her saying, that was definitely not one of them. And yet, it was so important. "Tommy Riviera."

"I'm sorry for his loss," she said quietly.

Sorry for Tommy's loss. Not John's. The distinction made all the difference in the world.

"I just spent the last couple months with his mother in Florida."

A slow smile spread on her face as she nodded her head. "Florida. With his mother."

There was something in her voice. Relief or bewilderment. He wasn't quite sure, so he cocked his head in question.

"You didn't go to Vegas, or drink alcohol out of a coconut," she said.

"Nope, no coconuts." Her random comment actually made him smile for a second. "My unit was tight. Really tight. And we'd made a promise to each other. If anything happened to one of us, the others would look in on their families. Make sure they were okay."

"I'm sure it was a great comfort to Tommy's mom to have you there."

"I hope so. I really hope so. I did some repairs on her house, fixed up her car, nothing big." He didn't mention he helped plan Tommy's funeral and then made sure his mom had a job and support system for when he left.

"You spent all three months in Florida?" she asked.

"No, I also stopped in North Carolina and Walter Reed Medical Center up in DC. I wanted to visit two of the injured men."

"That must have been incredibly difficult."

He nodded. "I have four more to stop in on, but they're all over the country. I need to map out a route to take."

"And then what?" she asked. "After you visit everyone and do as much as you can to help, then what?"

He rubbed the back of his neck and began pacing again. He hated this question, and it seemed like everyone wanted to know his plans. There was no way to figure out what would bring him some sense of peace and normalcy again.

"Hey," Vanessa said, popping up in front of him and interrupting his pacing. "I didn't mean to put you on the spot. I guess...well, I just wondered... Why can't you make Crescent Falls your home base?" She looked down at her clasped hands and a pink blush spread on her cheeks.

His body temperature quickly rose. Did she want him to stay? Once again he decided to answer with honesty. "I don't know."

With a nod, she returned to the crate she'd sat on earlier.

"My life is up in the air because I can't seem to get my feet under me. Does that make sense?"

"Absolutely."

"After all of that—the explosions and the loss—I came back here like a zombie. People were calling me a hero, but heroes save people. *All* the people," he amended quickly. "I put on a good face and shook hands with strangers. Accepted praise. But on the inside, I felt..."

"Dark?" she guessed.

He nodded, both surprised and grateful that someone finally got it. "Except at night. Nighttime is when you should be able to shut off your brain and quiet your mind. But for me, that's when everything explodes. I haven't slept in...I don't know how long." He ran a hand over his head. "When I close my eyes, it's all there."

"I'm sorry. I can't imagine what that's like."

He went back to pacing. "I don't ever want you to. I went through the motions every day. Until one night. *That* night. The night I came here and met you."

He stopped and turned around. She'd moved closer and was hanging on his every word.

"Really?" she asked.

He pushed a lock of hair behind her ear. A small gesture that he'd always wanted to do to a woman. Finally, he got his chance.

"You made the darkness go away. You brought the light."

• • •

Her knees were going to buckle. Any second now, she would be on the floor, deep in a puddle of gooeyness. Vanessa was a strong woman, but even she had a point where she couldn't hold out anymore. Who would blame her, either? Here was an amazingly good man who had just bared his soul to her.

But she'd been holding back all night. And he'd made himself clear. This needed to be her decision.

"I asked you if you would stay around Crescent Falls. I hope you will. Not just for me, and not just for your sister either. For you. Because you can travel all over the country chasing ghosts, or you can plant your feet here with your family. And I think you need that."

He let out a breath. Unable to contain her feelings any longer, she leaned toward him and pressed her mouth to his.

Once again, an electric jolt shocked her right to her core at the mere touch of his lips.

She waited for him to pick up the pace to their previous frenzied tempo. But John held back. He moved his lips over hers sweetly. His hands came up to frame her face but his touch was so light, so gentle.

His mouth was soft and his kisses felt like the barest hint of a feather trailing along her body, tickling her in the most delicious of ways. She leaned into him, urging him to take more. She would give him anything.

John pulled back. "Not fast. Not this time. I want to enjoy you."

"I thought you enjoyed me last time."

The corners of his mouth curved upward. "Oh, I did. But this time I want to take my time, make you realize how special you are."

"But...we're *here*." She gestured around the storeroom.

He shook his head and reached for her hand. Then he placed it, palm down, over his heart. "And you're here. I don't know how or why, but you are."

*Oh. My. God.* "You've gotta stop saying stuff like that."

"Then how about I do stuff like this?" With that, he pressed his lips to the side of her throat. She shivered.

"Or this?" he asked, and moved to the other side of her neck, running kisses up to her jawline.

"Or maybe this?" He framed her face, his thumbs running lazy circles on her cheeks. Then he kissed her. It obviously wasn't their first kiss, but somehow her breath caught and her stomach clenched as if it were. Goose bumps rose on her arms. His lips against hers felt that good. When he pulled back, he grinned. "Better?"

"Oh yeah. Much, much better."

One look into his earnest blue eyes and she knew he meant every single word that came out of his mouth. She felt every feeling he conveyed with his kisses and touches. Maybe she didn't have much—okay, any—experience with one-night stands, but she was pretty sure you weren't supposed to feel so connected to the person you slept with three months after the fact. But with every passing second, she wanted him more.

Should she tell him that? After all, he'd been nothing but honest with her. She wanted to tell him that she was amazed by him. That she couldn't begin to fathom what he'd been through, but she respected the hell out of it.

How many people completely shut down after they went through something like that? But he was honest and kind and generous. He'd come here to plan an engagement party for his sister. He'd spent months helping the mother of his fallen soldier. He made a point to check on the injured men from his unit. And she realized why he didn't want to stay in town, even if he didn't. By running around the country, taking care of everyone else, he didn't need to face his own issues.

Emotion swelled in her chest, and the enormity of it scared her. But where she would have recoiled in the past, she took one look into his handsome face and lost herself even more.

"Kiss me again, John."

He gathered her in his arms and pressed his lips to her cheek, her forehead, the tip of her nose, and finally to her mouth, running sweet, fluttery kisses along her lips until she was melting. Or maybe it was the fluid way he sank to the ground with her in his arms, changing the angle of the kiss to take it deeper.

He cradled her head and gently laid her back onto the floor. "Wait," he said suddenly. Popping up, he stripped off his shirt. Her breath caught at the sight of his amazing body. She began to reach out, wanting to run her hand from his broad shoulders over his toned chest and down to that defined waist, but then she realized what he was doing. He balled his shirt, lifted her head, and placed it on the soft cotton.

"This floor is so hard. Are you okay?"

She couldn't speak, and it took some intense, deep breaths to keep the tears that wanted to form at bay. The dichotomy of this man astounded her. This gorgeous, all-American soldier who'd seen so much more at the tender age of twenty-seven than most people would in their entire lives. Yet he could delicately hold her as if she were made of crystal and make her feel special and treasured.

"Vanessa?" he asked, leaning back.

All she could do was nod. He studied her for a moment, looking worried, but when she didn't shatter into a million shards of glass like he probably expected, he finally came to her.

And then their lips were sealed together and the kiss made her breathless. He ran his hands up and down her sides, eliciting sighs of pleasure she couldn't control. When he nuzzled her neck, she hugged him closer to her, wanting to absorb every inch of him.

She was so engrossed in how he was making her feel, she didn't even realize he'd removed her white waitress top, or that her skirt was on the floor next to her. All she was sure of was that his mouth was doing amazing things to her neck, her collarbone, then on down to one breast and then the other.

He brought her finger to his lips and kissed the tip, then trailed his mouth along her wrist and up her arm. Her eyes nearly rolled back into her head. The little nibbles and licks felt reverent, as if he were cherishing her instead of making out on a storeroom floor.

Tingles danced along her inner thigh as he moved his hand lower. He pressed his mouth to her belly and she laughed when he found her ticklish spot.

But her laughing stopped the second he found a more potent area. Before she realized it, he pressed himself to her and she reveled in the feel of his skin against hers.

She wanted to reciprocate, both for him and for herself. He'd explored every inch of her body, and she bit her lip just thinking about doing the same to him. But when she tried to push him back, to roll them so she could be on top, he stopped her, pressing her against the floor. As he did, she heard the crinkle of a condom and silently thanked him for having one on him.

He pressed a chaste kiss to her lips and shook his head. "This is for you tonight. This is all for you."

Overwhelmed, she felt a lump form in her throat, and her mind raced with thoughts of him. Only him. Then she didn't think at all when he slipped inside her.

They moaned in sync as he slowly moved, obviously in no rush to reach the finish line. This was so different than their one night together. Then, it had been hot and fast and intense.

But not now. This was hot, too, only in a completely

different way. This was all consuming, filling her with emotions she didn't know if she could comprehend.

And as John continued to move over her, she stopped trying to figure it out. She focused on him and what his body was doing to hers. That's when she could truly let go, falling over that beautiful cliff as his name burst from her lips. He followed shortly after with an exclamation of his own and a sated smile.

She wrapped her arms around him and he buried his face in her hair.

Vanessa had never felt happier.

# Chapter Nine

Something tore Vanessa out of a warm, wonderful dream.

Even though she should be beyond uncomfortable lying on the extremely hard floor of the dank, dark bar storeroom, she'd never felt more at peace. Maybe it was the fact that she was wrapped in John's arms as his chest rose and fell in a slow, comfortable rhythm. After everything he'd told her the night before, the sight of him resting warmed her heart.

She took stock of her body, wiggling her toes and shifting slightly. Her limbs felt heavy and used. At the reminder of the previous night's events, she let out a big smile as she pressed her face to John's bare chest. He smelled like pure man.

Some time during the night, she'd put her top and underwear back on and John had tugged his t-shirt over her head, surrounding her with his citrusy, ocean scent. He was still completely naked, covered only by an oversized beach towel they'd used for a Corona display a couple months ago. The sight of it made her giggle.

Then she heard a noise and froze. That's what had woken her up. Someone was on the other side of the door. Before she could wake John though, he popped up, eyes wide and muscles clenched.

"Did you hear that, too?" she asked, flinching at the wild expression he gave her when he heard her voice.

"Vanessa." He let out a long sigh and looked around the room. With a quick glance down at his completely naked self, he blushed, and she hid her smile. "Morning."

"Good morning." As she sat half-naked on the floor, hair mussed, breath already speeding up, he simply drank her in as a huge lascivious grin spread on his face.

Then he leaned down and kissed the crap out of her. And that's when the door to the storeroom flew open.

"Oh shit," Mike said as he quickly turned around and ran into the wall. Another man, wearing blue coveralls and carrying a toolbox, stood with his mouth agape as he took in the two of them. Clearly the locksmith had finally arrived.

"Mike," she yelped, her face growing hot. Vanessa quickly searched for her skirt and as she pulled it on, she realized that John was trying to shield her from everyone's view, the towel hastily tucked around his waist.

Mike turned from the wall, rubbed a hand over his nose, and averted his eyes yet again. "Shit," he repeated. "What the hell is going on? Are you okay?"

"We're fine. We got locked in last night by accident."

"Naked." That was the only word the locksmith said. Well, yelled at the top of his lungs was more like it. They all froze at his loud, raspy voice.

"Oh God, you don't have your clothes on," she said to John. She threw his pants at him and dragged her skirt up over her hips, ran a hand over her hair, and looked around for some kind of trap door or time machine. Mortified when she could find neither, she buried her face in her hands and groaned.

She could hear John moving around, hopefully pulling his pants on.

"We'll just give you two a minute." She looked up to see Mike grab the once-again-mute locksmith and yank him out into the bar.

John threw his sweater over his head, and she wanted to cry. Was her face as red as his? With this level of humiliation, it should be.

But she didn't cry. Instead, she snuck a glance at him. He nodded, his face composed and unruffled. Instantly, her skin began to cool off.

Somehow this man she'd only just met had the ability to make her feel calm when her life had become anything but in the last twelve hours. Without overthinking, she slid her arms around him and squeezed. Tipping her head back, she rose on her toes and pressed her lips to his.

When she pulled back he smiled. "What was that for?" he asked.

"A thank you."

He quirked a brow.

"For last night," she explained. "It was…amazing."

Running his hands up and down her arms, he offered another grin. "I'd like to see how you'd thank me if we went on a real date."

*So would I.* That was the problem, she realized, as they broke apart to finish dressing. They were never going to have a real date. The night was over and so were any chances of being together.

. . .

Five minutes later, Vanessa stood in front of Mike as he looked from her to John and back again.

"So, you're telling me that you cut your hand on broken glass," he gestured to the glass still littering the floor under the bar. "Then you went to get the first aid kit, this guy followed you, and the door closed by accident."

"That was my fault, actually," John said in a steady voice. He was much more pulled together than she felt at the moment. She'd had sex in the storeroom and got caught by her boss. Gah. How would she ever look Mike in the eyes again?

"I'm just glad you're both okay. When I got here and the front door wasn't locked, and then I saw broken glass, I gotta tell you, I almost had a heart attack."

"Sorry, man," John said.

"No, I'm sorry I didn't have that door fixed sooner." He gestured toward the storeroom, where the locksmith still appeared to be completely traumatized. She could relate. "Well, at least you guys found something to, uh, do."

"Ohmigod, ohmigod, ohmigod, ohmigod." Vanessa covered her eyes and willed this to all be some kind of messed-up dream. But when she peeked between her fingers, she found both men staring at her. "I'm so sorry, Mike."

To her surprise, Mike laughed, long and hard. "Trust me, you're not the first people to…let's just say, *utilize* the storeroom."

She let out a long breath. That made her feel marginally bett— "Wait, what?" she asked as his words hit home. *Ew gross.* Other people had had sex where they'd just been? She couldn't take much more of this humiliation.

But Mike only laughed harder.

One look at John showed that he was watching Mike, grinning ear-to-ear. But when he caught her furrowed brows and frown, he quickly composed himself.

"Don't worry about it, V. I'm just glad you're both okay and so sorry you got locked in there for the entire night." His gaze ran up and down both of them. "Actually, maybe I'm not too sorry." He winked. "In fact, maybe it wasn't so much of an accident…"

She threw her hands up in the air. "We didn't lock ourselves in the storeroom to have sex."

Mike cocked an eyebrow.

"Don't give me that look. Do you honestly think I would want to spend the night in that dirty, disgusting storeroom?"

"I think it probably wasn't so disgusting with this guy." Mike chucked a thumb in John's direction.

"I *am* quite charming," John added.

Now they were both starting to irritate her. Her head was pounding, her muscles were sore, and she was exhausted and in no mood for their mocking. "Oh yeah, you're right. We've been planning this little rendezvous for three months now. Hey, Mike — did you know we met right here at the bar?" She looked at John, expecting to see one of his somewhat cocky, yet still totally amazing, grins. Instead, he was frowning at something just over her right shoulder.

"Is that so?"

Her head whipped toward the door and the source of the soft, but disapproving, voice. With arms crossed at her chest and a scowl on her face, Jess's glare promised anger.

Lots and lots of anger.

"Jess, hey, come in," Mike called, oblivious to the tension.

"I'm fine right here."

"Meet John. He's—"

"My brother," she finished for Mike.

"Your brother. Your brother? Oh." Red flashed on Mike's cheeks as he looked from Vanessa to John and put everything together. He pointed toward the storeroom. "You know what? I better go check on the locksmith. I'm sure he needs help with something."

Mike left the bar area as quickly as humanly possible. Vanessa wished she could do the same. She'd never done anything like last night in her entire life, let alone stood half-dressed and fully mussed in front of multiple people.

"Jess, hey," John said.

Jess answered by narrowing her eyes and moving her hands to rest on her hips. If pouts could talk, hers would probably use a lot of four-letter words.

A pit formed in the deep recesses of her stomach, and for a moment, Vanessa couldn't breathe. She'd never felt worse in her entire life.

Stepping forward, she addressed her friend in a small voice. "Jess, I'm so sorry."

Jess turned on her, eyes blazing and a mad red flush reaching her cheeks. "I...I...don't think I can speak." With that, she turned abruptly and strode out the door.

Vanessa exchanged a quick, silent glance with John before they both took off after Jess. Once outside, the bright February sun pierced her eyes, blinding her after the dim lighting of the bar. Her meager excuse for an outfit did little to protect her from the elements. The biting wind and bitter cold would have taken her breath away even if she'd been fully dressed.

But that didn't matter. Right now, she needed to get to Jess and explain. Spotting her near the stone bridge, she grabbed John's hand and they ran in that direction.

"Jess, please wait. Let me explain."

Jess turned, ready to say something. But her mouth closed as she glanced down at their joined hands. Pointing, she let out a loud huff. "What is this?"

Vanessa snatched her hand back as if John was poking her with a branding iron. "Nothing. It's nothing."

"It's not nothing," John said, his voice clear and steady.

What the hell? He wasn't helping. She threw a look in his direction but he didn't seem to catch on to the gravity of the situation.

"I'm sorry, but it's not nothing," he repeated.

"Then what in the hell is going on here?" Jess demanded.

"We didn't plan any of this. John showed up at the bar last night and we got locked in the storeroom by accident."

"But I heard what you said in there." Jess pointed back at the bar. "You told Mike that you met three months ago. The only guy you met three months ago was... Oh God."

"Jess," Vanessa said.

"Your one-night stand? My brother? Yuck! Yuck, yuck, yuck," she said, shaking her head with her eyes closed.

Vanessa knew the feeling. She wished she could close her eyes for the rest of her life, but she was pretty sure her eyelids had frozen open. She blew on her hands, trying to create enough heat to warm her body...and maybe the atmosphere in general, which had turned downright frigid.

Jess leveled a glare at her brother. "What are you even

doing here?"

John frowned. "Your engagement party, of course. I came here to see you."

She scoffed. "Funny, but I don't recall living in Mike's Bar. You get to Crescent Falls and instead of finding your sister—your only family—you go to a bar and hook up?" Jess shrank into herself, her lips trembling. "You hooked up with my *best friend*, Jack." Swiping at her eyes, she let out a shaky breath. "I feel like such an idiot."

The anger had drained from her voice, leaving only pain. Vanessa's heart ached at the sight. She'd never meant to hurt her best friend. "You're not an idiot," she said, rubbing her arms again. Maybe she'd freeze to death and Jess and John could go on like nothing happened.

John must have noticed. "Can't we go back inside to have this conversation?"

Thankfully, Jess didn't argue. Within seconds, they found themselves in the blissfully warm lobby of Vanessa's apartment. Not the best place to have this conversation, she realized, trying not to look at the mailboxes. Maybe they could go upstairs and calmly talk things over while sipping something hot and soothing.

Wishful thinking.

Jess glared at her brother. "So you guys...met...three months ago?"

"Funny story," John said.

Jess rolled her eyes. "How funny?"

"I introduced myself to Vanessa as John, but she only knew your brother as 'Jack' from the stories you told."

"Right." Vanessa stepped forward, hope swelling in her chest. "I didn't put it together. How could I? I assumed John and Jack were two different people."

"And I had no idea the super-hot woman I met was your best friend."

Jess looked back and forth between them, her frown deepening.

"We didn't know who the other was when we first met," John tried again. "Honestly."

"I believe you." And she looked like she did. Then her face fell. "But you figured it out before you got locked in the bar. Didn't you? You knew after that. And you still did... whatever you did in there." She held up a hand. "I don't even want to know."

She had them there. Vanessa silently willed herself out of the situation, but no matter how hard she tried, she was still standing in her lobby, wearing disheveled clothing, and trying—but failing—not to remember exactly what they'd done three months ago against the mailboxes behind Jess.

She was scum. Total and complete, fungus-infected, mucus-filled, reprehensible scum.

Jess's voice broke the silence. "I am beyond weirded out right now. I have to go."

"Jess, wait," Vanessa called at her friend's retreating back.

"I can't," Jess called and ran toward her car.

John stepped forward and rubbed his hands up and down Vanessa's arms. "I am so sorry."

Vanessa searched his magnetic blue eyes, wishing they held the answer she needed. The answer she wanted to hear. They didn't. Couldn't. Because she'd just hurt her best friend—her *family*—and the one guy she wanted was the source of all the trouble.

She stepped back, immediately missing his touch. "We

can't do this. Not now, not ever. Jess is too important to me. And she should be too important to you, too."

John sighed. "She'll come around. I know my sister. We just need to give her time."

"No, I've ruined everything."

"You haven't. Besides, this thing that's between us, well, I'd really like to explore it."

Equal parts horrified and ecstatic, she backed up even more. She wanted nothing more than to throw herself into his arms and let him take care of her, erase the memories of this wretched morning.

But in the end, it wouldn't matter. Even if she gave in to John now, he would still leave. How many times had he said he wouldn't stick around? Not only would she lose him, she'd lose her best friend.

He pulled her to him. "Do you feel what I'm feeling?"

Of course she felt it. But she couldn't tell him or they'd be upstairs and in her bed before she could remind herself why it was a bad idea.

"Do you?" he urged.

*He's leaving. He's leaving. He's leaving.*

That shouldn't have hurt as badly as it did. Not after spending just two nights with the guy, but there it was. She swiped away a tear and then met his gaze. "It doesn't matter what I feel because you're not sticking around."

His face fell. "Vanessa…"

She held up a hand. "Don't. You're leaving. You said so yourself. Focus on fixing things with your sister, not me."

Before he did something to change her mind, Vanessa ran up the stairs to her apartment and away from the most amazing man she'd ever met.

# Chapter Ten

John wanted to run after Vanessa. Hell, he knew which apartment was hers—though even if he didn't, he wasn't above knocking on every door until he found her. But what she'd said stopped him.

*You're leaving. You said so yourself.*

She was right. He had no plans to stay in Crescent Falls after his sister's engagement party—if Jess still wanted him there at all. Of course, he would be back for her wedding.

John pushed through the door and out into the cold. The bridge loomed in front of him, reminding him of the night he'd met Vanessa, of how scared he'd been that she planned to jump. The thought of seeing another person die—let alone the beautiful, sad woman he'd watched from across the bar—had turned his blood to ice.

He stopped in the exact spot he'd first kissed her, sucked in a lungful of icy air, and let it out in a long, slow exhale, watching his breath turn into a smoky haze in front of his eyes. Three months was a long time, and yet they'd fallen back together like he'd never left. Connections like theirs didn't happen every day.

He looked up at Vanessa's apartment and thought he saw movement in the window. When he peered closer, there was nothing.

*You're leaving.*

He *was* leaving. So why did the reminder make him feel so moody? Pain bloomed behind his eyes, throbbing like a drumbeat. He rubbed his temples. It was probably from sleeping on the cold, hard floor.

At least he'd slept. When was the last time he'd gotten that kind of deep rest?

Maybe it was just the first of many restful nights. Maybe when he got where he was going, things would get better.

John turned on his heel and headed toward his car, running a hand over his face. As he drove to his sister's townhouse, he took in Crescent Falls. Main Street must be the town center. Mike's Bar was at the far end, near the stone bridge. From there, he passed a grocery store, a library, some small businesses, a flower shop, and a couple of restaurants, then small, but well-kept houses with big porches. There were trees everywhere, and evidence of kids and families by the swing sets and toys littering the tidy lawns.

It seemed like a nice little town. Safe. Clean. The kind of town that made him remember why he'd proudly given years of his life to protect and serve.

He shifted in his seat as he turned into Jess's driveway. Her brick townhouse was narrow but looked like it stretched up three levels. She had two gray planters out on the front stoop, but it was too cold for anything live at this time of year so they sat empty. But he could imagine how welcoming it would appear with multi-colored flowers overflowing from them.

He just hoped that welcome still extended to him.

He took the steps that led up to her front door two at a time. After his quick rap on the door, it opened, with Jess standing there silently, watching him.

"Can I come in?" he asked.

Stepping back, she opened the door wider and he crossed the threshold. He followed her toward her combination kitchen, dining area. They stood on opposite sides of the table.

He ran a hand through his hair. "Look, I know you're mad—"

"You got that right." Then it was like the air was let out of her. She slumped into a chair and looked up at him. "But you have no idea why I'm mad."

He didn't? John joined her at the table. "What's up?"

She looked all around the table before her gaze met his. When it did, her eyes filled with tears. "I was so afraid I would never see you again."

"Because of what happened with Vanessa?" he asked.

She glared at him and swiped at a tear. "No, you idiot. Because of you being in Afghanistan for the last couple years. My God, John, I've been terrified."

*Shit*. Not knowing what else to do, and never good at handling female tears, John rose and went to his sister. He wrapped his arms around her. "Don't cry, Jess. I'm fine. I'm right here."

"Finally." The word was muffled since Jess had put her head against his chest. But he still heard it. He got the message.

He leaned back and tapped his sister's nose. "I should have come here first. I'm sorry."

She offered a small smile. "Thanks. Do you want something to drink or eat or anything?"

"Both would be great. But I think we need to talk first."

Jess got up, retrieved a box of tissues, and then rejoined him at the table. "So, you and V, huh?" She didn't meet his eyes.

"We didn't know who each other were when we met."

After a long moment, Jess said, "I know."

"But you should also know that it probably wouldn't have mattered. I like her."

Unmoving, Jess stared at him, her face a mix of emotions, none of which he thought would bode well for him.

"Vanessa said something about how us getting together would be repulsive to you."

"It is. Duh." She stuck her tongue out and rolled her eyes. "It's…icky."

"Another word she used," he said.

She scrunched her nose and the corners of her mouth turned up. "But you and Vanessa getting together isn't the worst thing in the world."

"It's not?"

She shook her head. "Nope. I can think of a lot of things that would be worse."

"Such as?" he asked.

"Never seeing my brother again."

And John suddenly realized the root of the problem. He covered his sister's hand with his. He thought about what Vanessa had tried to tell him when they were in the storeroom, about his sister needing someone. Jess always had everything together. Even when she was young, she was organized and in control. He'd assumed she'd been fine since their mother's death.

He'd wanted at least one of them to be okay. And *he* sure as hell wasn't fine with the events of recent years.

"Jess," he began, trying to figure out how to tell her about his time in the Army without really telling her about it. "The things that happened to me when I was in Afghanistan were horrible. I don't want you to know about them."

"Why not? Because you don't think I can handle it? I have news for you." She reached across the table and shoved a finger into his chest. "I'm stronger than you think. More than that, I'm your only family. That means you're my only family, too. And families share. Families support each other. So stop being such an idiot and tell me."

With her stubborn chin jutting out, and the fire in her eyes, he wanted to laugh. But he kept himself in check because he knew she was serious. More than that, she was right.

"Okay," he said. Then, for the second time in twenty-four hours, he talked about everything that had happened. Jess asked questions from time to time, and he had to stop a couple times when he felt too overwhelmed.

Jess made them coffee and breakfast. The scrambled eggs were fluffy and tasted just like their mom's. When he told her that, they both cried. And then they cried some more while recounting all the old family stories they could remember.

The strange part was that sharing all of it didn't have the negative effect he'd always assumed it would. Instead, he actually started to feel better.

"Don't you have to go to work?" he asked.

"And miss this? I've gotten more out of you this morning than the first twenty-seven years of your life combined." Her smile lit up her blue eyes. "Besides, the advantage of owning your own business is you can play hooky when you want."

"In that case, I have an idea," he said, and Jess cocked her head. "Why don't we spend some time together? Just the two of us."

Her eyes lit up. "Seriously?"

"Yeah. Me, you, a movie fest, lots of junk food. Double Stuf Oreos still your favorite?"

A tear spilled over her cheek. "Damn," she said, running a hand over it. "How many times are you going to make me cry today?"

"This is the last time, I promise. Unless your choice for a movie is *The Notebook*. I know how your gender just loves to cry at that one." He cringed. "Please don't pick *The Notebook*."

Laughing, Jess jumped up from the table and threw her arms around his neck. "Thank you." When she pulled back, she looked at him intently. "I just wish we could do this more often."

Something had shifted in the last couple of hours. It had been subtle so he hadn't realized it until that very moment. But he knew what he needed to do. What he wanted to do.

"Maybe we can. I mean, if you wouldn't mind having a roommate until I find my own place in town."

She blinked. "In what town?"

"Crescent Falls."

"What? Ohmigod! Are you serious?"

He shrugged. "Seems like a pretty nice place to live. I

mean, I'll have to figure out what I want to do for work. And I might have to go to a different town to get a beer since Mike might never allow me back inside and—"

She cut him off by jumping up and giving him another long hug. "My hero."

For the first time in months, John liked the sound of that.

# Chapter Eleven

Vanessa stripped off her clothes and threw them in the trash. After all, she didn't plan on wearing her bartending outfit again anytime soon. Then she got in the shower and stood, unmoving, under the warm, pounding water.

She didn't know what aspect of the last twelve hours to focus on. Her brain kept replaying both Mike and Jess's reaction to finding her and John together. Her body was firmly settled on remembering the way John's kisses and touches had made her feel. But her heart…it couldn't help but think about John and Jess.

She toweled off and began to run a comb through her wet hair, her rose-scented shampoo permeating the small bathroom. Jess and John had lost so much. Not only John's loss in Afghanistan, but also their mother. Jess was a tough cookie, but Vanessa knew she'd been having a rough time lately. After all, she'd just gotten engaged and hadn't had any family to share that happy news with.

She knew the feeling.

Before she could talk herself out of it, she picked up her cell phone, found the number she was looking for, and hit send.

A refined, if not somewhat prim, voice answered on the third ring. "Well, this is a surprise."

Vanessa walked to the window, her hand tightly clutching the phone. "Hi, Mom."

"Why aren't you at work?"

Vanessa imagined her mother glancing down at the fancy gold watch she always wore. She would be dressed in some kind of pastel outfit that included a full suit, or at least a blazer. Her outfit would be topped off with a light spritz of Chanel No 5. The fresh, crisp scent always reminded Vanessa of her mom.

She took a deep breath. "Actually, I lost my job."

"What?" Her mother's voice took on a high-pitched tone.

"I lost my job three months ago."

"Three months? And I only get a call now. That's lovely, Vanessa. What happened?"

"Downsizing."

"Didn't I tell you not to move to that little town?"

"They were happy with my output and I liked working there. I've been working at a restaurant ever since, to keep the money flowing in." Strategically, she decided to leave the bar part off of Mike's Restaurant and Bar.

"Well, I suppose you'll be wanting to move home. I'll have Rosa make up your old room."

Her skin began to heat. An angry outburst was right around the corner. Only, she didn't want to fight with her mom. That's not why she'd called.

"I'm not moving home. I found a new job and I start on Monday. It's a couple of towns away but it's not much of a commute."

"Oh."

Was she mistaken or did Vanessa detect a hint of disappointment in that small, little word?

"So you don't want to come home. Then why did you call?"

"Because I wanted to hear your voice. Because you're my mom. And even though you're not happy with the choices I've made in life, at least you're around to disapprove." She ran a hand through her hair. "I realized recently that I'm lucky to have you. Not everyone is as lucky."

Her mother's voice hitched. "Oh, Vanessa."

Vanessa took a deep breath. "I'm sorry I disappointed you."

"Vanessa Lucille Hewitt."

She snapped to attention, the way she always did when her mom pulled out her full name and said it in that no-nonsense brisk tone, and braced for whatever scolding was to come.

"How could you think for one second that I'm anything less than proud of you?"

Blinking, Vanessa gripped the phone tighter. "But…you can't be. The way you always talk to me…"

"Oh, it may not come off as proud. I suppose I get my delivery from *my* mother." She sighed loudly. "Nevertheless, you are an accomplished, beautiful, talented woman. I may not always agree with your choices, but I always support them."

Vanessa found herself standing in the middle of the room, her mouth hanging open. "Really?"

"Absolutely."

She blinked. The conversation wasn't going the way she'd expected at all, but she wasn't going to argue with the words she'd spent a lifetime wishing she'd hear. "Will you come down here for a visit? I'd like you to spend some time with me in Crescent Falls. You've never seen my apartment or the town. I think you'd really like it. And, um, it would be really great to spend some time together. Just me and you."

The phone line was silent for a few moments and Vanessa held her breath. Finally, she heard a sniffle.

"I'd love that," her mother said.

Relief filled her body and she sank onto the couch.

"Now, what about your art?" Her mom had returned to her usual business-like self. Vanessa would have smiled, only she didn't really want to talk about her art.

"There's nothing going on with my art." *As usual.*

"You are so incredibly talented, Vanessa. And before you interrupt me—like you always do—and talk about those idiots at your college, I'm going to stop you. I know they said you never put enough emotion into your work. But that's only because you've never tapped into it. It will come. You are talented," she repeated.

Vanessa walked to the kitchen and riffled through her purse. When she found one of the papers she'd doodled on the night before, she studied it. John had said she was talented, too.

She leaned against the counter and looked at the unfinished painting in the living room. Her mother's voice was mixing with John's in her head.

*You are talented.*

She thought about how she felt right at this moment. The impromptu conversation with her mother made her feel lighter than she had in a long time. Like everything was right in the world and she didn't have to try so hard.

Then there was John. He may not be staying in Crescent Falls, and maybe their meeting was never meant to be a long relationship, but it had been impactful. When she thought about him she wanted to cry at his leaving. At the same time, the memories of their time together made her stomach flutter and her pulse race. It was a light-hearted, floating sensation that felt incredibly satisfying.

Again, she glanced at her easel. Just like that, she began walking toward it, her breath coming out in short spurts as excitement took over.

"You know what, Mom? I never thought I would say this. But…I think you're right."

A small chuckle sounded. "Ah, well, I could have told you that years ago."

# Chapter Twelve

Vanessa made her fourth cup of coffee of the day — an all-time caffeine high, even for her. She added her usual cream and sugar and let out a huge yawn. Hardly surprising, considering she hadn't slept at all the night before.

Although she had to admit, the lack of sleep had been worth it. After talking to her mom, she begun painting like never before. Everything felt so clear. From the colors to her brushstrokes, emotion had poured out of her when she put paintbrush to canvas.

So much so, that she'd been able to keep thoughts of her best friend and her best friend's brother at bay. But now that the sun was setting and she was finally taking a break, she couldn't stop thinking about them. Especially after that call with her mom. Feeling helpless, she could only worry about any kind of conversation they may, or may not, have had.

God, she hoped they talked. She still felt so horrible at seeing her best friend so upset.

She'd sent a text message to Jess yesterday apologizing and asking if they could talk in person. Jess hadn't responded. She couldn't blame her.

"I won't crush on your brother," Vanessa said out loud. "Great job, V." Irritated with herself, she took a long swig of coffee, even though it was hot and burned her throat. That's what she deserved anyway.

A knock on the door pulled her out of her thoughts. She ran a hand through her hair, but knew it wouldn't help. After an entire night of painting, her hair was a lost cause.

Her best friend stood in the doorway wearing a tentative smile and looking fresh and rested. Vanessa was equal parts jealous and impressed.

Neither of them said a word. They both seemed to be taking the other in. Finally, at the same exact time, they both blurted out, "I'm sorry."

"You're sorry?" they also said in unison.

Jess laughed and Vanessa pulled her inside the door. "Get in here already. What in the world are you sorry for?" Vanessa asked as Jess shed her coat and walked into the living room.

"I got your text yesterday and I didn't write back."

Surprised, Vanessa collapsed onto her super comfortable couch. "Ohmigod, Jess, don't worry about that." She waved a hand in the air. "I understand. I'm shocked you're even here now after what I did."

"You hooked up with my brother," Jess said, taking a seat next to her.

Vanessa looked down at her rug, deciding it really need-ed a good vacuum, while she figured out what to say. "Jess," she said, her voice hitching. "I'm really sorry. I know I said that I would never—"

Jess held up her hand and smiled. "You hooked up with my brother. You didn't kill my brother, or do some kind of harm to me."

"I didn't?"

Jess laughed. "No, of course not. I mean, knowing, um, all that I now know about Jack is kind of making me want to gouge my eyes out or look into memory erasing. But you're my best friend."

Vanessa could only stare at her. "But I had a one-night stand with *your little brother*."

"Technically, you had a *two*-night stand with him."

"I'm so sorry," Vanessa said again.

Jess pointed at her. "Stop saying that," she said in a firm voice. "I have to ask you something important. Do you want to date Jack? Sorry, John."

Vanessa froze. The truth was, she couldn't stop thinking about him. She hadn't been able to stop since that first night. After their time in the bar, she felt like she was going to explode. More than anything, she wanted to feel his touch and hear his voice.

"It doesn't matter," she said to her best friend. "He's not going to be here anyway."

"Hypothetically, what if he did live here?"

Vanessa shrugged. "He doesn't."

"I will play the wounded best friend card if you don't answer my damn question. If the situation were different, how would you feel about my brother?"

Vanessa swallowed, her mouth suddenly dry. How much should she reveal? In the end, she decided to go with the truth. Her best friend deserved that. "I really like him, Jess.

It doesn't make any sense. I barely know him. But…"

"But what?" Jess prompted.

"I miss him. When I'm with him, I feel beautiful and smart and like the best version of myself. I know it started as a one-night stand…"

"But it's gone way beyond that now," Jess finished for her, offering a big, genuine smile. "I think he feels the same way about you."

Vanessa looked at her hands. Paint flecks dotted her skin. "Like I said, though, it doesn't make any difference. Even with your blessing, John's leaving." She sighed. "I wish…"

"What do you wish?" Jess asked after a couple seconds.

"Let me show you." Vanessa rose and walked to her easel. She'd set it up near the window that overlooked the stone bridge. She grabbed her canvas and brought it back to the couch.

Jess gasped, her eyes widening as she took in the finished painting. "V, ohmigod! Did you paint this?" She peered closer. "It's amazing."

"Really? You think so?" She suppressed the urge to twist her hands together.

"Yes. Are you kidding me? It's so beautiful, but sad, too. Sad in a really great way. God, it makes me feel so much all at the same time."

That was exactly what she'd been going for when she'd painted the two people on the stone bridge, their hands outstretched, fingers almost touching, but not quite. At the same time, an ominous fog was beginning to form.

Jess's reaction was exactly what she'd always wanted to hear from her art teachers and mentors. She offered a half-smile. "I'm going to enter this in the art show next week."

"Really? You're going to enter the art show?"

"Someone kinda believed in me enough to make me realize I should."

"Oh, V." With that, Jess threw her arms around her. "I'm so, so proud of you." They hugged for a long time, relief filling the air. "Your painting, it's you and my brother right?"

Vanessa nodded but stayed quiet.

"I have something I have to tell you." Jess took a deep breath. "Something really wonderful happened yesterday."

Vanessa placed her painting on the coffee table. "Yesterday? You mean when you found out your best friend and your brother—"

"After that." Jess laughed. "I got my brother back, V. John and I spent the entire day together. We talked and laughed and cried. We watched movies and ate junk food."

"I'm so happy for you."

Jess reached for her hand. "There's more."

Vanessa waited, wondering what else could have possibly happened.

"He's staying. My brother's going to live here."

Her mouth fell open and tingles raced over her body. She shook her head. No, she must have heard wrong.

"I'm serious," Jess said. "He's going to live in Crescent Falls." She jumped up. "And now that we know how you really feel, you can be with him."

Hope bloomed in her chest. "Are you serious?"

"Not gonna lie, it's still kind of weird for me." Jess hugged her. When she pulled back, she said, "But I love you, V. And this isn't about me. Go be with my brother."

"But...but...maybe he doesn't want to be with me." She bit her lip, nerves overtaking her.

"I'm pretty sure that isn't true. You know how I know?" Jess pointed to the window. "Go check it out."

Vanessa walked to the window and pushed the curtains back. She didn't see anything out of the ordinary down on the street. Then her eyes fell on the bridge. That's when she saw him, bundled up in a brown leather coat.

Her heart actually fluttered.

She spun around. Jess had a huge smile on her face. "Well, go on. Someone is waiting for you."

She didn't have to tell her twice. Vanessa snatched her coat from the hook by the door and flew down the steps, two at a time, and pushed open the main door.

But as she stepped onto the street, Vanessa took a moment. She was still wearing her oldest, most cruddy pair of yoga pants. The ones she wore when she painted, which made them even worse. She must look disgusting. For a second, she contemplated running upstairs, but then John turned and spotted her.

Her heart stopped. He was so damn handsome.

She walked toward him, excited and scared at the same time. Her pulse picked up, and the closer she got, the faster it beat. "Hey," she offered.

"Vanessa," he said simply.

His deep voice sounded like heaven.

"John, I…it's so…I mean…" She cut herself off by chewing on her lip. All she'd thought about for the last three months was this man. And now she was standing in front of him, with his beautiful eyes watching her intently and that strong jaw twitching as he waited for her to say something. It made her knees feel weak.

Taking a step closer, she tried again. "John, all I want—"

He cut her off with the most amazing, comforting, secure hug ever. Cocooned in his arms with her head nestled in the crook of his neck, all of the angst and heartache vanished.

"God, you feel good."

"Jess just told me," she said, leaning back just far enough to look him in the eyes. "You're staying in Crescent Falls."

"You were right. My sister does need me. And if I'm being honest, I need her, too." He kissed her forehead. "And I need *you*."

He took her lips and she twined her arms around his neck, holding tight.

His kiss was temptation. She moaned into his mouth, wanting more. His answering groan left her shaking with need—the need to hold him, the need to feel his body pressed against hers, the need to share…everything with him.

When they finally broke apart, she smiled up at him. "I want to be with you," she said. "I want to see where this goes."

His eyes shone. "That is one mission I very gladly accept."

She ran a light finger over his cheek, reassuring herself that he was real. That this moment was real. "I can't believe this all started with one night together."

"One night that will lead into many, many more nights if I have anything to say about it."

With that, he pressed his lips to hers again. *You were supposed to be my Mr. Wrong*, she thought. But as they stood, wrapped in each other's arms, kissing on the bridge where they met, the water dancing below and the stars twinkling above, Vanessa knew that Mr. Wrong turned out to be just right.

# Epilogue

John took a look at the quaint three-bedroom brick house with the large wraparound porch and massive oak tree in the front yard. It seemed like only yesterday he'd driven down this street for the first time and noticed it.

Who would have thought that he'd eventually buy it? He was a homeowner. He was living in Crescent Falls.

He was happy.

What a difference six months could make.

"Standing around again?" Vanessa asked. "Thought the Army trained its soldiers for hard work."

He smiled. "Hard work? Sure. Face down enemies, help the good guys, never give up. However, the Army seemed to have left off moving boxes upon boxes of…how many pairs of shoes do you own exactly?"

"You're about to find out. Still ready to live together?"

Any other option was unacceptable. He planted a soft kiss on her lips and handed her the top box. Together, they crossed the threshold.

They placed the shoeboxes at the bottom of the staircase. "Coffee break?" she asked.

He raised an eyebrow.

"Your sister set up my Keurig this morning," she explained.

"In that case, I'd love some." He leaned back against the counter and watched her move around the room, snagging two mugs and digging the k-cups out of an open box. The idea that he was going to see her do this every single morning brought a huge grin to his face.

"What?" she asked.

"Nothing. Where is my sister anyway?"

"She's with my mom. They ran to the store after Jess said I was forbidden to put any dishes in the cabinets without lining them with shelf paper first. Naturally, my mother wholeheartedly agreed." She shrugged. "Figured it was easier to just let her do it than argue."

John chuckled. "Probably. It's been great living with her the last couple of months, but I have to admit that I won't miss her overly anal organizational skills. She yelled at me last week when I put one of her towels on the wrong shelf. Apparently guest towels do not mix with everyday towels." He took the mug of hot coffee she handed to him. "What about you? Are you going to miss your apartment?"

She smiled and put another K-cup in the coffeemaker. "A little. What I'm really going to miss, though, is being able to stumble upstairs after a couple glasses of wine at Mike's."

"I think I can help you stumble the two blocks to this house."

"I'm counting on it. Oh, by the way, your phone was

ringing earlier. Lance," she added and took a sip from her cup.

"No kidding? Must mean he's stateside again. I'll give him a call later. Try to convince him to swing by Virginia." He'd love a visit from his best friend.

"I can't wait to meet him. But in the meantime, we need to get back to unpacking. I have another art show next weekend. Plus, we really need to get things in order if you want to visit a couple more of the men from your unit before September, Mr. Campbell."

"You just love calling me that."

She leaned against the counter beside him and nudged his shoulder with her own. "Hey, you need to get used to it. You're going to be the best sixth grade teacher ever."

*Holy shit. I'm going to be a sixth grade teacher.* He would be responsible for shaping young minds. What in the hell had made him decide to do this?

John glanced at the woman standing next to him. Every time he accompanied her to one of her art shows, he watched her confidence grow. Without a doubt, her courage to put herself out there had inspired him to try this new venture.

"I'm nervous." He hadn't meant to say it out loud. But one thing he'd learned over the last six months was that Vanessa had broken down all of his walls. With her, he was nothing but himself.

"They are going to love you. The girls will be smitten and the boys will be impressed. After all, how many kids get a teacher who is a real life Army hero?"

He cocked an eyebrow and she laughed. But he took a moment to enjoy the fact that he no longer cringed at the word hero. In fact, he liked that she thought of him that way.

He liked the idea of being her hero.

That's why he knew that the ring box burning a hole in his pocket was the best idea he'd had since he'd decided to move to Crescent Falls. Now he only had to decide when to ask her to marry him.

Because she was his hero. And together, they would make this their home.

# Acknowledgments

A lot of this story was written and worked on very late at night. Even in the wee hours, it did not escape my notice that two other people were up working late as well. Heather Howland, you are an amazing editor and I can't believe how hard you work. Nicole Resciniti, I can't believe how lucky I am to have you as an agent and friend. Thank you both for all of the help and support, especially late at night. It didn't go unnoticed!

A huge thank you to the people at 2300 Wilson for your unwavering support, enthusiasm, and encouragement. Seriously. Most writers aren't as lucky as me.

Thank you to my friends. I know, writers are crazypants. I can be crazypants. That's why your support means so much to me. Quite frankly, you all might be crazypants for being my friend. Smoochies!

Big glittery thank yous to my critique partners, Lynne Silver (extra glitter) and Carlene Love Flores (Hero) for everything. And an extra special thank you to Adrian Flores for the Army help. Also, hey, Dana Rodgers - you rock!

Glitter toss to my family, especially Mom, Dad, Kevin, Danielle, Baby C, and all of my cousins.

And a huge kiss to my fur-baby Harry. Thank you for loyally sitting next to me while I type this, as well as loyally sitting next to me every single day. No matter what.

To all the readers out there – you are amazing!

# About the Author

Kerri Carpenter began writing in her grandmother's kitchen at the age of seven in a small town outside of Pittsburgh, PA. A life-long fan of reading, she got lost in the worlds of The Baby-sitters Club and Sweet Valley High. She also assumed that everyone had characters and plots forming in their heads at all times. Once she turned to romance novels, she couldn't get enough of books with happy endings, so she started writing her own. Now, Kerri writes contemporary romances, usually set in small towns. She enjoys reading, cooking, watching movies, taking Zumba classes, rooting for Pittsburgh sports teams, and anything sparkly. Kerri lives in Northern Virginia with her adorable (and mischievous) poodle mix, Harry.

Kerri can be found online at her website, on Facebook, and Twitter. Or, sign up for her newsletter.

*Also by Kerri Carpenter...*

### FLIRTING WITH THE COMPETITION

Lawyers Whitney March and Jordan Campbell are interviewing at a prestigious law firm. For the same job. And Jordan is determined to win, despite his sexy, capable, and fiery rival. But when the elevator they're sharing comes to an abrupt stop, they're stuck—*together*. The only thing they have in common is determination to get the job...and an unexpected and escalating attraction. And it's only a matter of time before these competitors indulge in a very sexy little connection between floors.